P9-DHT-559

MUD CITY

DEBORAH ELLIS

{*}{*}{*}

Mud City

A GROUNDWOOD BOOK
DOUGLAS & McINTYRE
TORONTO VANCOUVER BERKELEY

Groundwood Books / Douglas & McIntyre
720 Bathurst Street, Suite 500, Toronto, Ontario M5S 2R4
Distributed in the USA by Publishers Group West
1700 Fourth Street, Berkeley, CA 94710

We acknowledge for their financial support of our publishing program the Canada Council for the Arts, the Government of Canada through the Book Publishing Industry Development Program (BPIDP), the Ontario Arts Council and the Government of Ontario through the Ontario Media Development Corporation's Ontario Book Initiative.

National Library of Canada Cataloging in Publication
Ellis, Deborah
Mud city / by Deborah Ellis.
ISBN 0-88899-518-0 (bound).–ISBN 0-88899-542-3 (pbk.)
1. Kabul (Afghanistan)–Juvenile fiction. 2. Refugee camps–Pakistan–Juvenile fiction. I. Title.
PS8559.L549M83 2003 jC813'.54 C2003-902660-4
PZ7

Design by Michael Solomon
Cover illustration by Pascal Milelli
Printed and bound in Canada

To children lost and wandering,
far from their homes.

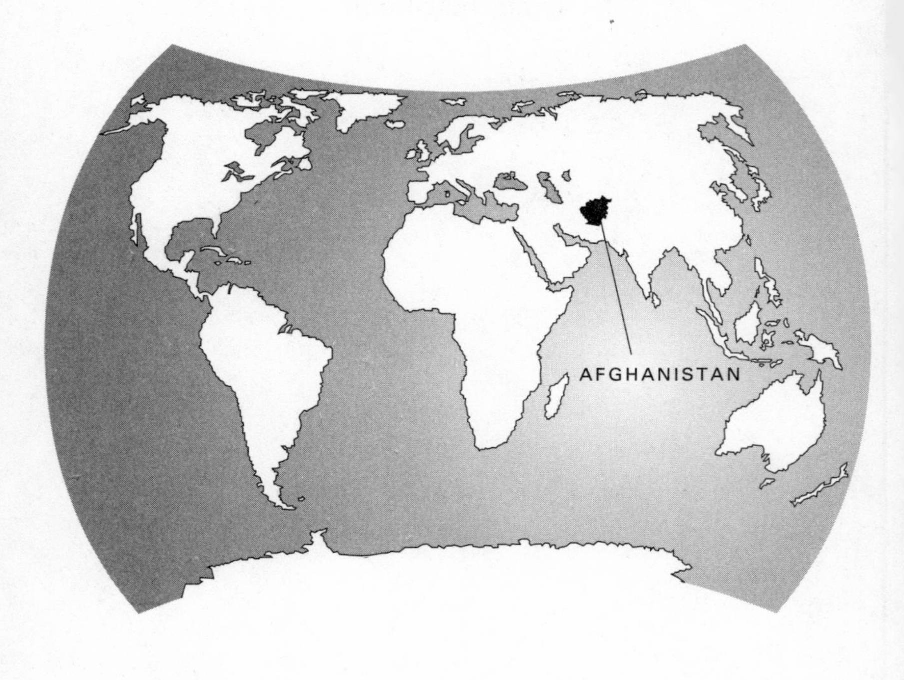
AFGHANISTAN

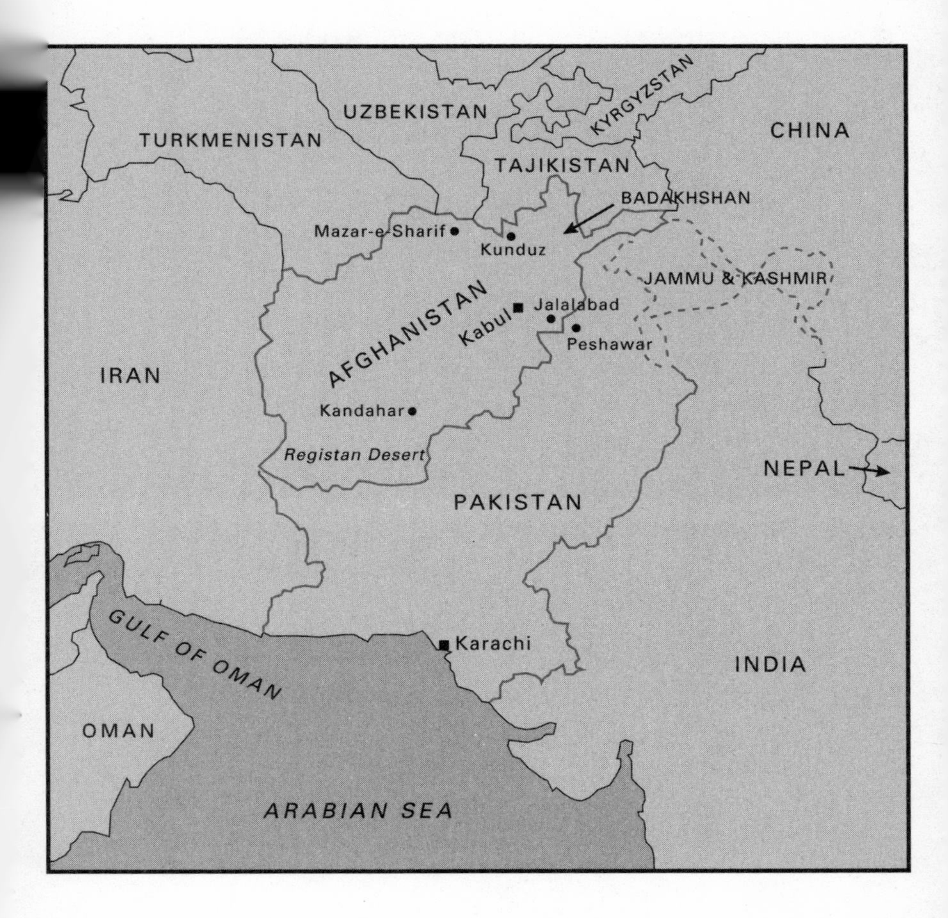

UZBEKISTAN
KYRGYZSTAN
CHINA
TURKMENISTAN
TAJIKISTAN
BADAKHSHAN
Mazar-e-Sharif
Kunduz
JAMMU & KASHMIR
AFGHANISTAN
Jalalabad
Kabul
Peshawar
IRAN
Kandahar
Registan Desert
NEPAL
PAKISTAN
GULF OF OMAN
Karachi
INDIA
OMAN
ARABIAN SEA

ONE

"When did Mrs. Weera say she would be back?"

Shauzia had asked that question so many times that the woman in Mrs. Weera's hut didn't even look up. She simply raised an arm and pointed at the door.

"All right, I'm going," Shauzia said. "But I'm not going far. I'll sit in the doorway until she comes back."

But the woman at the makeshift table was absorbed in her work. Not only was this the office for the Widows' Compound, the section of the refugee camp where widows and their children lived. It was also the office for a secret women's organization that operated on the other side of the Pakistan border in Afghanistan. The Taliban were still in power there. Mrs. Weera's organization ran secret schools, clinics and a magazine.

Shauzia was tempted to jump onto the table

and kick the papers onto the dirt floor, just to get a reaction. Instead, she went outside and plunked herself down beside the doorway, her back slumped against the wall.

Jasper, her dog, was taking up most of the sliver of shade by the hut. He lifted his head a few inches off the ground in greeting, but only for a moment. It was too hot to do anything more.

The streets and walls of the camp were all made of mud, which soaked up the heat like a bread oven, baking everything inside, including Shauzia. Flies landed on her face, hands and ankles. Nearby, the resident crazy woman rocked and moaned.

"Remember when we were in the high pasture?" Shauzia asked Jasper. "Remember how cool and clean the air felt? How we could hear birds singing, not women moaning?" She reached under her chador to lift up her hair, which was sticking to the back of her neck. "Maybe we should have stayed with the shepherds," she said, brushing off a fly and redraping her head and shoulders with the chador. "Maybe I should have kept my hair short like a boy's instead of letting it grow back. That was

Mrs. Weera's idea. Mrs. Weera orders me around, has dumb ideas, and won't even get me a decent pair of sandals. Look at these!" She took off a sandal and showed it to Jasper, who kept his eyes closed. The sandal was barely held together by bits of string.

Shauzia put it back on her foot.

"It's not fair for you to be in this heat, either," she told Jasper. "You're a shepherding dog. You should be back in the mountains with the sheep or, even better, on the deck of a big ship, next to me, with the ocean wind all around us."

Shauzia wasn't completely sure whether there was wind on the ocean, but she figured there must be. After all, there were waves.

"I'm sorry I brought you here, Jasper. I thought this place would be a stepping stone to some place better instead of a dead end. Do you forgive me?"

Jasper opened his eyes, perked up his ears for a moment, then went back to his nap. Shauzia took that as a yes.

Jasper used to belong to the shepherds, but as soon as he and Shauzia met, they realized they really belonged together.

Shauzia leaned back and closed her eyes. Maybe she could remember what a cool breeze felt like. Maybe that would cool her down.

"Shauzia, tell us a story!"

She kept her eyes closed.

"Go away." She wasn't in the mood to entertain the compound's children.

"Tell us about the wolves."

She opened one eye and used it to glare at the group of youngsters in front of her.

"I said go away." She never should have been nice to them. Now they wouldn't leave her alone.

"What are you doing?"

"I'm sitting."

"We'll sit with you." The children dropped to the dirt, closer to her than was comfortable in this heat. A lot of them had shaved heads because of a recent outbreak of lice in the compound. Most had runny noses. They all had big eyes and hollow cheeks. There was never enough food.

"Quit butting into me," she said, pushing away a little girl who was leaning on her. The orphans Mrs. Weera was always finding and bringing into the compound were especially clingy. "You're worse than sheep."

"Tell us about the wolves."

"One story, then you'll leave me alone?"

"One story."

It would be worth the effort, if they really did go. She needed some quiet time to plan out what she was going to say to Mrs. Weera. This time, she wouldn't be put off by a request to do one of those "little jobs."

"All right, I'll tell you about the wolves." Shauzia took a deep breath and began her story.

"It happened while I was working as a shepherd. We had the sheep up in the high pastureland in Afghanistan, where the air is clean and cool."

"I can make Afghanistan with my fist."

"So can I."

A dozen grubby fists were thrust into Shauzia's face. The thumbs were stuck out to represent the skinny part of the province of Badakhshan.

"Don't interrupt. Do you want to hear the story or not?" Shauzia said, waving the hands away.

"We were up in the pastureland, where

everything is green – grass, bushes, pistachio trees, great oak trees – a beautiful green."

Shauzia looked around for something to compare it to. The compound was all yellowish-gray mud. Most of the children had spent their whole lives there.

"Look at Safa's shalwar kameez. Up in the high pastureland, the whole world is green like that." There was green under the dirt of Safa's clothes. The water supply was low, and no one had been able to do laundry.

The children oohed and aahed and started babbling about colors. Shauzia had to shut them up so she could finish the story. Then maybe they'd leave her alone.

She pictured the pastureland in her mind and, for a moment, she was taken away from the noise, dirt and smell of the refugee camp. "I was sitting up with the sheep one dark night, guarding them, because sheep are so stupid they can't look after themselves. The other shepherds – big grown men – were asleep. I was the only one awake. I sat by a small fire, watching the sparks fly up into the sky like stars.

"There was an eerie silence in the hills. All I

could hear was the sound of the shepherds snoring. Then, suddenly, a wolf howled!"

Shauzia howled like a wolf. Some of the children gasped and some of them laughed, and the women in the embroidery group nearby stopped chatting for a moment.

"That was followed by another howl, and then another howl! There was a whole pack of wolves in the forest, wanting to gobble up my sheep.

"I stood up and saw the wolves begin to creep out from the shelter of the trees. They wanted to eat the sheep, but first they had to deal with me. I counted four, then five, then six – seven giant wolves coming toward me, tense on their haunches, ready to spring.

"I bent down and grabbed two burning sticks from the fire. I held them up just as the wolves jumped at me. They were hungry and strong, but I was angry that they had disturbed my quiet night, so I was more than a match for them. I kicked at them and waved the burning sticks until they were so tired out that they collapsed at my feet and fell asleep. In the morning, they were so embarrassed, they simply slunk away back into the forest, grateful that I didn't laugh at them."

"Hello, children!" Mrs. Weera swept into the compound like a strong wind. "Every time you tell that story, you add another wolf," she said, whooshing past her into the hut.

Shauzia jumped to her feet and followed her inside.

"Mrs. Weera, I need to talk to you."

"Another one of our secret girls' schools has been discovered by the Taliban," Mrs. Weera was saying to her assistant. "We must see what we can – "

"Mrs. Weera!"

But Mrs. Weera ignored Shauzia.

Shauzia felt Jasper's solid dog-body beside her, and it gave her strength.

"Mrs. Weera, I want to be paid!" she shouted.

That got Mrs. Weera's attention. "You want to be paid? For telling stories? Whoever heard of such a thing?"

"Not for telling stories."

Mrs. Weera was already striding away on those strong, phys-ed teacher legs of hers.

"Mrs. Weera!" Shauzia shouted. "I need to be paid!"

Mrs. Weera came back. "Which is it? Want or need? I'm sure we all want to be paid, but do we need to be? And are you not already being paid? Did you not eat today? Will you not sleep under a roof tonight?"

I will not back down this time, Shauzia vowed to herself. "I told you my plans when I first came here. I told you I'd need to earn some money, but you've kept me so busy with your little jobs, I haven't had time to look for real work."

"I would have thought bringing comfort to your fellow Afghans in a refugee camp could be considered enough real work for a lifetime."

"A lifetime!" Shauzia exclaimed in horror. "You expect me to do this for a lifetime? I didn't leave Afghanistan just to live in mud!" She flung her arms at the mud walls surrounding the Widows' Compound, knowing that on the other side of them in the regular part of the refugee camp were more mud walls. Maybe the whole world was mud walls now, and she'd never get away from them.

Mrs. Weera gave Shauzia a hard look. "This isn't that France nonsense again, is it?"

"It's not nonsense."

"She thinks she'll just go to the sea, hop on a ship, sail to France and be welcomed there with open arms," Mrs. Weera announced to the growing crowd that had gathered to see what the excitement was. As others laughed, Shauzia realized that was what she hated the most about living in a refugee camp. She couldn't even have an argument in private.

"She wants to spend her life sitting in a cornfield!" Mrs. Weera continued.

It's a lavender field, Shauzia thought, but she didn't bother saying anything. And I don't want to spend my life there. I just want to stay there long enough to get the sound of your voice out of my head.

"Why won't you go into the nurses' training program like I arranged for you? In a few years, you might be able to work as a nursing assistant and earn money that way. The sea isn't going anywhere. Neither, as far as I know, is France."

"A few years? I can't spend a few years here! I'll go crazy! I'll be like her!" Shauzia pointed at the crazy woman. A woman with no name, she had been found rocking and moaning on the streets of Peshawar. Aid workers had brought her to the Widows' Compound. She still rocked and moaned but, as Mrs. Weera said, "At least she's safe here from the beatings the street boys gave her."

"Shut up!" Shauzia yelled at the woman, unable to stand the noise any longer. The woman ignored her.

"Use some respect in your voice when you speak," Mrs. Weera said sternly. "Why can't you be more like your friend Parvana? She always spoke most respectfully."

Parvana didn't like you any more than I do, Shauzia thought, but again, she kept her mouth shut. Mrs. Weera, she'd discovered, had the talent of hearing only what she wanted to hear.

"If you can't pay me for the work I do here, I'll have to leave and find work that will pay me money."

Mrs. Weera's voice softened. "You don't know what it's like out there. You've always been taken care of. You won't be able to manage on your own."

"What do you mean, I've always been taken care of? I've always taken care of myself! My family certainly didn't take care of me." An unwanted image came into Shauzia's mind, of coming home after a day of working in the streets of Kabul to a dark, crowded little room, to people saying, "How much money did you make?" instead of "How are you?"

"Your family, flawed though they were, also waited for you to come home every evening. You earned money to buy them food, but they cooked the food for you and provided you with a place to be each night. When you lived in the mountains, the shepherds watched out for you, and now all of us in the Widows' Compound watch out for you."

"Watch out for me? You don't even get me proper sandals like you promised. All you do is boss me around. Why don't you go back to Afghanistan and boss the Taliban around instead of me?"

"Shauzia, stop this. You are far too old to be acting like a child."

"Then stop treating me like a child! Stop treating me as though I were one of them!" Shauzia gestured toward the group of small children who were following the argument with open-mouthed delight. She suspected they found it even more entertaining than her wolf story.

Mrs. Weera took a deep, slow breath. "You want me to treat you like an adult?" she said calmly. "All right, I will. As an adult, make your choice. If you decide to stay here, you stay without complaint. You will contribute your time and talents to the best of your ability, without expecting money, because you'll understand that there isn't any. If you decide that life here is not for you, you know where the main gate of the camp is. We have enough problems helping those who want our help. Take a few days to think about it, then give me your decision."

Shauzia was stunned into silence. She stared hard at Mrs. Weera, and Mrs. Weera stared hard right back at her.

"I don't need a few days to think about it," Shauzia said coldly, hoping she sounded braver than she felt. "I'm leaving tomorrow, and I'm going to find a great job and become rich, and go to France, and never come back here again!"

"Very well," Mrs. Weera said quietly. "We'll have a farewell party for you tonight."

With that, she walked away.

TWO

There was no escaping the sound of Mrs. Weera's snoring, and by now Shauzia knew better than to try. She used to put a pillow over her ears, or toss and turn and make loud sighing noises, hoping to wake Mrs. Weera, but nothing worked. Mrs. Weera slept the way she did everything – full out – and she didn't waste time worrying about whether she was bothering anyone else.

Shauzia sometimes went to another hut to sleep, but Mrs. Weera's hut gave her something no other place did – a little bit of privacy. Shauzia slept on a toshak spread out under the table. A blanket hung over the side of the table created a tiny, private space.

"It doesn't keep the snoring out," she said to Jasper, who usually slept with her. "But it does make me feel like there is some place in the world that is mine."

Shauzia lay awake in her little room late on

the night after Mrs. Weera left her in the courtyard. The rest of the day had gone from bad to worse.

At Shauzia's goodbye party that evening, everyone in the compound ate together around the cook fire in the courtyard. Mrs. Weera made a speech about how much she had appreciated all of Shauzia's hard work.

"I know Shauzia will be successful in reaching her goal of getting to the sea, and of building a fine new life for herself in France." She went on to talk about how beautiful she had heard France was, and how she was sure Shauzia would have a marvelous time wandering through the cornfields.

All the time she spoke, Shauzia's fists were tightly clenched in anger.

After Mrs. Weera had finished talking, the other women also said nice things about Shauzia. How helpful she was, how clever, how they knew she had a brilliant future ahead of her.

And then the children piped up.

"Don't go, Shauzia!" they cried, the little ones sobbing and crowding in on her. "Stay and tell us stories!"

Shauzia was furious. She knew Mrs. Weera had staged this party to make her want to stay in the refugee camp.

Then Mrs. Weera said, "I have good news, Shauzia. I've arranged a job for you in Peshawar. You will be a housemaid in a women's needlework project and daycare center. You can live at the center, and the job will pay enough that you'll have a bit of money to save even after you pay for your rent and food. Isn't that wonderful? Plus, I'll be able to come and visit you every week when I meet with the project. I'll take you there tomorrow and help you get settled."

The other women applauded and talked about how lucky Shauzia was, but Shauzia was seething.

She was still seething as she lay on her mat, with Mrs. Weera's snores all around her.

"She thinks she can control everything," she whispered to Jasper. "She thinks she can control me."

She remembered her first day at the Widows' Compound. She had been wandering around the camp after being dropped off there by the shepherds, and was directed to the compound by an aid worker.

As soon as she walked through the door in the compound wall and saw Mrs. Weera, she wanted to back out, but it was too late.

"I know you!" Mrs. Weera exclaimed in her loud, booming voice. Everyone in the compound stopped what they were doing and stared at Shauzia. "You're Parvana's little friend."

Mrs. Weera had been a physical education teacher and field hockey coach before the Taliban closed all the schools for girls and made the female teachers leave their jobs. She had lived with Parvana's family in Kabul for awhile. Shauzia remembered how bossy she had been then, and wasn't surprised that she was still bossy.

In a few strides, Mrs. Weera's long legs crossed the courtyard. She stood in front of Shauzia. Shauzia could imagine what the older woman saw – a skinny girl whose face carried on it months of living out in the sun and the wind, clothes filthy and tattered, but with her back straight and her head up high.

"You stink of sheep," Mrs. Weera said, "but we can fix that. And I see you still look like a boy. We can fix that, too." She hollered out an order for hot water and girls' clothes.

"I'd rather keep looking like a boy," Shauzia said. "If I look like a girl, I can't do anything."

"Nonsense," Mrs. Weera said. It was a word Shauzia was to hear her use many times. "The Taliban are not in charge here. I am. Oh, you have a dog, too." She bent down and peered intently at Jasper, who wisely took two steps back. "A most adequate dog," was her verdict.

She turned away, and Shauzia allowed herself a small smile of relief. Mrs. Weera obviously didn't remember how angry she had been with her the last time they had met in Kabul.

The smile came too soon.

"You left Kabul without a thought to how your family would survive without you."

"They didn't like me!" Shauzia yelled. "They were always shooting, and they were going to marry me off to some old man I didn't even know, just to get some money. I meant nothing to them!"

"You don't abandon your team just because the game isn't going your way," Mrs. Weera replied. "Now then, before you get settled, I have a little job for you."

Shauzia had been doing Mrs. Weera's little jobs ever since.

"No more," she told Jasper. "And I won't be a housemaid for her, either. I don't need a house to sleep in. I slept outside with the shepherds. I can sleep outside in the city. Then all the money I make can go toward getting to the sea."

She reached under her pillow, where she kept her most valuable possession – a magazine photo of a lavender field in France. She couldn't see the picture in the darkness, but she felt better with it in her hand.

That was where she needed to be, in a field of purple flowers, where no one could bother her. She would sit there until the confusion left her head and the stink of the camp left her nostrils. When she had had enough of that, she would go to Paris and sit at the top of the Eiffel Tower until her friend Parvana joined her there, the way they had promised each other. They would spend the rest of their days drinking tea and eating oranges and making fun of Mrs. Weera.

She pushed herself up on her elbows. "Let's leave tonight," she said to Jasper. He thumped his tail, and that was all the encouragement she needed.

She got up and groped around in the corner until she found the bundle of her old boy clothes. She changed into them. Then she grabbed a fistful of hair and, using the scissors from the table top, cut and cut until the hair on her head felt short again. She put on her cap, tossed the blanket shawl around her neck and picked up her shoulder bag. She didn't have any other belongings.

Resisting the urge to yell "Goodbye!" in Mrs. Weera's ear, Shauzia quietly left the hut with Jasper right behind her.

They passed the hut used for embroidery training, and the one used to teach older women how to read. They doubled as sleeping huts for some of the families.

Shauzia went into the food storage hut. There wasn't much there, but she took the few pieces of nan left over from the day's meals and wrapped some cold cooked rice in a bit of cloth. She put the food and a small plastic bottle for water in her shoulder bag.

Back out in the courtyard, she looked around the compound one last time. Everything was quiet except for the sound of Mrs. Weera's snoring and, farther away, the sound of someone crying outside the Widows' Compound.

There was no reason to stay. The camp was dark. Shauzia began to regret her decision to go off in the middle of the night. But before she could talk herself out of it, she turned and walked through the compound door and continued on her journey to the sea.

THREE

There was a loud honk from behind. Shauzia jumped out of the way, and a huge truck roared past her. The exhaust fumes made her cough.

Jasper stuck close to her legs – so close that she was finding it difficult to walk. She could feel him trembling.

"It's all right, Jasper," she said, patting him, but she was feeling pretty shaky herself.

It had been dark when they walked away from the refugee camp, and they had kept walking right through dawn. Now the day was in full swing, and the closer they came to the nearest city, Peshawar, the crazier the traffic became.

The highway was clogged with every type of vehicle. There were buses so full that men clung to the outsides, and little three-wheeled cars that looked like toys zooming in and out of traffic. They were all brightly painted, with many colors and designs. There were white vans and taxicabs and regular cars. It seemed to Shauzia that they were all honking their horns at the same time.

They shared the road with motorcycles that had whole families piled on them, and bicycles loaded down with parcels. There were carts pulled by horses, donkeys, buffalo and even a camel. Shauzia watched an old man use all his strength to pedal a bicycle loaded down with lumber. The bike teetered and weaved and was almost run into by a passing bus.

It was too much. Shauzia took Jasper to a shady spot under a tree. They sat and watched the traffic speed by while they caught their breath.

"I wonder if we made a mistake coming here." Shauzia said. "I didn't think it would be so noisy. I didn't think it would be so... confusing." She scratched Jasper behind one of his ears, more for her comfort than for his.

"Maybe we should even have stayed with the sheep," she said. "At least the air was easier to breathe, and not so hot. Besides, the sea is such a long way away. What if we never make it? We'll be stuck here."

Jasper nudged her hand so she would keep scratching.

"Do you think we'll make it?" she asked him. He wagged his tail and licked her face.

Shauzia took the photo of the lavender field out of her pocket and looked at it for what was probably the millionth time.

"This is where I'm going," she said, more to herself than to Jasper. "And to get there, first I have to be here."

She put the picture back in her pocket, stood up and took a deep breath full of gasoline fumes.

"Let's go," she said to Jasper. Then she grinned. "I'll pretend to be a mighty warrior, like that Ghengis Khan who conquered Afghanistan. I'll invade this puny city. Nothing stands in my way!" She swaggered back to the highway in what she imagined was a Ghengis Khan strut, got honked at again and resumed her journey along the side of the road. She went back to being just Shauzia, but at least she was moving forward.

"I remember trucks and cars from Kabul," she told Jasper, keeping her hand on his head to reassure him. He was still trembling. "All you've known is sheep. Don't worry. You'll get used to this."

Jasper wasn't so sure. He darted away at the sound of every horn or loud rumble. Shauzia was afraid he would get confused and run into the traffic instead of away from it. When she spied a length of blue binding twine on the ground, she picked it up, tied part of it around Jasper's neck and used the rest as a leash.

"It's for your own good," she said. "Just until you're not scared anymore."

Jasper scratched twice at the rope. Then he licked Shauzia's cheek, and they started to walk again.

"There are so many Afghans here, it looks like Kabul," she said. Even the market looked like Kabul's market, with fruit piled high on outdoor platforms and skinned goats hanging on hooks. Butchers fanned newspapers over them to keep the flies away.

Two things were different, though. One was that although some women wore the burqa, others had their faces showing, and no one beat them for it.

The other thing that was different was that

all the buildings were intact. No bombs had fallen here. Shauzia had lived among bomb rubble all her life. It felt strange not to see any.

"There must be lots of ways to make money here." Shauzia doubted Jasper could hear her in the noise of the crowd, but she spoke to him anyway, just to have someone to talk to.

All around her, boys her age and younger were working. She saw them in auto repair shops, pounding metal at a blacksmith's, selling oranges off a cart and carrying trays of tea. She saw boys hanging off the sides of buses. They hopped off and urged in customers, taking their money, then climbed back onto the railing as the bus pulled away from the curb. She passed a construction site and saw small boys covered in dirt, leading donkeys loaded down with bricks.

Languages swirled around her. She recognized the Afghan languages – Pashtu, Dari and Uzbek – and she heard others, too, that she thought must be the Pakistani languages.

The crowd got thicker, and Shauzia kept a good grip on Jasper's leash.

A foul-smelling, slow-moving river divided the two sides of the market. Shauzia saw shops that sold jewelry and canned goods. She saw a shop that sold nothing but burqas, lined up on the walls, hanging like blue ghosts. Everywhere there were people selling goods off trays and karachis.

Shauzia walked around the market looking at all the shops and trying to imagine herself working in them. When she was too tired to walk anymore, she found a place on the ground in a bit of shade from a building and leaned back against the wall. Jasper sat beside her. She took out her plastic bottle, drank some water and poured some in her hand for Jasper. They shared a piece of the bread she'd brought with them from the camp. Then they each drank more water, to wash down the bread.

It was good to eat and drink. Shauzia felt completely worn out. She closed her eyes to rest.

"This is my spot."

Shauzia opened her eyes. Standing in front of her was a woman covered by a burqa.

"This is my spot," the woman said again. "I come here every day."

"I'm just sitting," Shauzia said.

"Sit somewhere else."

Too tired to argue, Shauzia and Jasper got to their feet.

The woman took their place. “Help me,” she begged to a passerby, who ignored her. “Just one or two roupees?” she called to another.

“Do you make much money that way?” Shauzia asked.

“Maybe ten roupees a day.”

“Is that a lot?”

“It’s enough to keep my children hungry.”

“Maybe if you lifted your burqa so people could see who you are... ” Shauzia suggested.

“What do you know?” the woman replied angrily. “I keep my face covered when I beg so that no one can see my shame. I was an office manager in Afghanistan. I’ve graduated from university. And now look at me! No, don’t look at me! Go away!”

Shauzia stood there for a moment feeling awkward that she’d hurt the woman’s feelings, and angry that the woman had made her get up just when she had gotten comfortable. Finally, since she didn’t know what to do with either her awkwardness or her anger, she just walked away, and Jasper went with her.

The woman had scared her. If someone who had been to university was reduced to begging, what hope did Shauzia have?

She knelt down beside Jasper and pretended to fuss with his leash. She kept her head low so no one could see her crying.

"I don't like it here," she whispered. Jasper licked at her tears. Shauzia hugged him close. Then she stood up and kept walking.

There were a lot of beggars in the market. Some were women, covered and uncovered. Some were sick people with twisted limbs. Others were children her age. People walked past the beggars' outstretched hands as if they were invisible.

"The people they're begging from look as poor as they are," Shauzia said. She turned away. It was all too awful to watch.

They walked through the market again.

I've got to ask someone for a job, she thought, but each time she got close to approaching a shopkeeper, she felt too shy to do it.

"You can't possibly manage on your own," Mrs. Weera had said. Shauzia remembered how everyone had laughed.

She took a deep breath and headed to the nearest shop, a bookstall.

"Give me a job!" she demanded of the man behind the stack of books.

She was quickly ordered out of that shop, and away from the four other shops she went to.

The day slipped away. The market stayed open after dark, but the bare lightbulbs hanging here and there from poles and wires created weird, frightening shadows in the streets. Shauzia and Jasper squeezed themselves into an alcove between shops. She could tell from the smell that they were sharing the space with decomposing fruit and other garbage, but at least they were out of the way of people, cars and shadows.

She leaned against the wall, missed Mrs. Weera's snoring, and fell asleep sitting up.

Shauzia woke to a gray predawn morning, her head pillowed on a pile of rotting cabbage. Jasper was already awake, chewing on something he had found in the garbage.

She got up and they went to a water tap she'd seen in the market. She threw water on her face, and she and Jasper had long drinks. The water filled up her belly – for awhile.

She spent the day looking for work. Many of the shopkeepers told her she was too dirty to work in their shops. Others already had all the help they needed.

The sun was starting to go down when she passed a butcher shop, almost empty of meat, full of dirt and dried blood.

"Your shop needs cleaning," she said to the butcher, who was sitting on a stool just inside the doorway and drinking a cup of tea. "I could clean it."

The butcher swallowed a mouthful of tea, looked her up and down and said, "This is a man's job. You're a small boy. Go away."

Shauzia didn't budge. "I can clean your shop," she said again. She put her hands on her hips and stared right at him. She was hungry and tired and not in the mood for nonsense.

The man drank some more tea and swirled it around in his mouth before swallowing it.

"That's a fine dog," he said finally, nodding at Jasper. "He looks hungry."

Of course he's hungry, Shauzia thought. So am I.

"Wait." The butcher disappeared into the shop and came out again with chunks of meat on a piece of newspaper.

"That's good meat," the butcher said, rubbing

Jasper's ears while he gulped down the meat. "Good meat for a good dog." He stood up. "Be here early in the morning. I'll give you half a day's work cleaning the shop. You do a good job, and I'll pay you. You do a bad job, and I'll toss you out." He disappeared into the shop, but appeared again a moment later. "You can bring your dog," he said, before disappearing for good.

"Thank you," Shauzia called after him. She knelt down and threw her arms around Jasper.

"I have a job!" She felt like singing.

She had to have something to eat. As soon as Jasper was finished with the meat, they went to the bread bakery, which was starting to close up.

"If you let me have a piece of bread tonight, I'll pay you for it tomorrow," she said. "I'll have a job in the morning."

The baker picked up a loaf of nan from a small stack and tossed it at Shauzia. She wasn't expecting it, and it landed in the dirt. She quickly picked it up.

"How much do I pay you tomorrow?"

"Go away, beggar. I've given you food, so go away."

Shauzia's face burned with shame. She wasn't a beggar.

She opened her mouth to say something, but changed her mind. She might need free bread again.

She shared the bread with Jasper. Then they both had a drink of water at the tap. The food felt good in her stomach.

The marketplace was quiet. All the stalls were shut down. Shauzia saw people sleeping in the shadows and doorways.

She and Jasper went back to the butcher shop. It, too, was closed. They settled down in the doorway.

"This way, I'll be sure to be on time for work in the morning," she said. The doorway smelled funny, but she was so tired that she fell right asleep.

FOUR

Shauzia woke to the sound of the butcher unlocking the iron grill over his shop.

"Your dog will get too hot out here," he said. "Bring him through to the back. There's a pan on the shelf. Give him some water."

Shauzia and Jasper followed the butcher through the shop to a small cement yard in the back. There was just enough room under an awning for Jasper to stretch out in the shade.

Shauzia found the pan, filled it with water and took it out to Jasper.

"Wait here for me," she said. "If I do a good job, maybe he'll give me more meat for you, or at least some bones for you to chew."

"Clean the shop," the butcher said. He showed her where the bucket, brushes and cleaning solution were kept. "I'm going to go out to have my breakfast now. I'll be back soon to check on you."

Shauzia got to work. She worked quickly,

washing down the empty shelves and trays where the meat would go when it was delivered. She wasn't bothered by the dried blood. One of her jobs as a shepherd was to pick up sheep dung and flatten it into cakes. They used the cakes for fuel when they couldn't find wood.

That had been a nasty job. Dried blood was nothing.

If the man liked her work, he might have other jobs for her.

The disinfectant he told her to use smelled strong but clean.

Shauzia had an idea.

She took the bucket into the little walled yard, stripped off her clothes, washed herself all over with the clean-smelling water, then quickly washed her clothes as well.

"I know I look funny," she told Jasper as she put on her shirt that was wrung out but still wet. "It will dry, and at least I'm clean enough now for people to hire me."

She got back to work.

"Spilled a bit of water on yourself, I see," the butcher said when he returned from his breakfast. He nodded at the work she had done and poured her a cup of tea from the thermos he had filled at the tea shop. "Take some bread," he said, pointing to a small stack of nan wrapped in newspaper.

Shauzia tore a loaf in half and took half out to Jasper, who gulped it down, then sniffed the ground for more.

"Maybe later," she said, and he thumped his tail.

By the time she had finished the job, the heat of the morning had almost dried her clothes.

"Do you have any more work for me today?" she asked.

"Not today. I am closed today, so there will be no deliveries or customers. You are a hard worker. Maybe I will have jobs for you from time to time. I just said maybe," he added, when Shauzia's face lit up. "Fetch your dog, and I will pay you."

Shauzia got Jasper.

The butcher peeled a ten-roupee note from a bundle he pulled out of his pocket. He hesitated for a moment, then added another ten-roupees.

"Take the rest of the bread," he said. She did.

"Look," she showed Jasper. "Three loaves.

We'll eat like kings today and still have some for tomorrow. Food, money and clean clothes, and we only just got to the city! This will be easy."

But she had no more luck that day, or the next. The day after that, her sandals fell apart. She tied them together with a bit of twine that she found on the ground, but that only held for a half a day. It wasn't just the straps that were broken. She'd worn one sole clean through to the pavement.

"I can't go on like this," she said, looking at the bloody mess the bottom of her foot had become.

They sat at the side of the road for a good long while, wondering what to do.

In the middle of the afternoon, a pedlar with a karachi full of rubber sandals pushed his cart slowly past her.

"That's what I need!" Shauzia called for him to stop and walked gingerly over to him, her bare feet tender against the hot pavement.

"How much for a pair of sandals?" she asked.

The pedlar named a price. It was more than Shauzia had in her pocket.

"I don't have enough." She felt like crying. Her bare feet burned. She had to hop from one foot to the other.

The pedlar watched her for a moment, then rummaged in the bottom of his cart. Finally he handed her several sandals that did not match.

"Try these," he said. Shauzia tried them on until she found a sandal to fit each foot. One was brown, and one was green.

"Why do you have all these sandals that don't match?" she asked.

"People with one leg need sandals, too," he replied.

"How much for these?"

"How much do you have?"

Shauzia showed him the money in her pocket.

"That will do," he told her. He took it all.

Now she had sandals, but she had no money.

"It's all Mrs. Weera's fault," she said to Jasper, as they watched the sandal man wheel his cart away. "If she had got me new sandals like she was supposed to... " Shauzia didn't complete the thought. Blaming Mrs. Weera suddenly seemed like a waste of time. There was never any money in the compound for things like sandals.

"What do I do with these?" she asked Jasper, holding up her old torn sandals. She decided to leave them on the sidewalk. She put them down, but before she had taken a few steps, a young man swooped down and picked them up.

Maybe she should have kept them after all.

Shauzia slept in a different spot each night for the first few nights she was in Peshawar. The city was never quiet at night. There were always the sounds of gunshots, arguments and trucks. There were sounds that could have been crying and could have been laughing. Sometimes it was hard to tell the difference.

When people passed by they ignored her, or stared down at her. Sometimes they dropped trash on her. She told herself it was because they didn't see her. The more it happened, though, the harder that was to believe.

One day, after she and Jasper had been in Peshawar for more than a week, Shauzia found a good sleeping spot between two buildings, off a quiet street. It was a sort of a shelf, big enough for her and Jasper to sleep on.

“This will make a good home for us,” she told Jasper.

In a nearby garbage dump she found an old cardboard box. She tore it up and used the pieces to line the cement shelf.

She sat on the cardboard to test how it felt.

“We’ll be the most comfortable sleepers in the city,” she said to Jasper, who joined her on the bed and wagged his tail.

Shauzia stepped up her job search. She did many different jobs, some lasting a few days, some just a few hours. In the cloth market, with rainbows of fabrics hanging over the walkway like a multicolored forest, she helped unload bolts of cloth and sorted buttons into jars.

She did a bit more work for the butcher, cleaning the shop again, and one day she set up sheep’s heads on the table outside the store. He gave her a good-sized bone for Jasper at the end of that day. He also recommended her to his friend with a grocery store, and she got a day’s work there, cleaning the place.

Everywhere she went, she saw groups of small children dragging blue plastic sacks, poking through garbage.

"I'll do that if I have to," she told Jasper, "but I don't see how I could make much money that way."

She got a few days' work as a tea boy while the tea shop's regular delivery boy was sick. This was work she had done in Kabul, delivering trays of tea in metal mugs to merchants who couldn't leave their shops for a break. She was good at it, too, and could rush through the narrow streets of the market without spilling a drop. Everywhere she took tea, she asked if there was work for her. She was rewarded with a job sweeping out a furniture warehouse.

One day, instead of looking for work, she went down to the train station.

"Do any of these trains go to the sea?" she asked the man behind the ticket counter.

"You want to go to Karachi," the man said.

"Karachi," Shauzia repeated. "Like the cart. Is it expensive?"

"Return?"

"One way."

The ticket seller told her the price. It was much, much more than she had saved in her money pouch. She thanked him and headed out. She was almost back on the street when some people going on a journey gave her a few roupees to help them carry their bundles.

After that, on the days when she didn't have other jobs, she went to the train station and carried people's bags for tips. She couldn't go there often. There were men whose regular job was to be porters, and they chased her away if they saw her.

It was just as well. She found it hard being at the station, watching other people get on the trains, heading off on a trip.

When would it be her turn?

"I work cheaper than the other porters," she told Jasper one evening. "Some day, someone is going to work cheaper than me, and I won't be able to get work there anymore. The problem is, there are so many of us. There are a lot of Afghans here, and we all need money."

Each night, she added more roupees to the pouch hung around her neck. Each night, she was a little bit closer to the sea.

One day, she saw her reflection in a store window. Her hair was getting long. She was starting to look like a girl again.

She went to one of the barbers who set up

shop along the edge of the sidewalk. She sat down on the bit of cardboard he'd placed on the cement to make customers more comfortable. Beside him, in a little box, were his scissors, brushes and razors, and a little mirror so people could check out his work when he was done with them.

"I'd like my hair shaved off," Shauzia told him, and they agreed on a price. She wouldn't need to get it cut again for a long time.

While he was working, the barber joked about giving Jasper a shave, too. The jokes were not very funny, but it made Shauzia feel better about losing her hair.

She avoided her reflection after that, but her head was a lot cooler.

When she got to France, she would grow her hair again, she promised herself.

Each evening, she bought food to share with Jasper out of her day's earnings. On hard days, when she didn't earn much money, she bought only bread. On better days, she bought meat patties from a street vendor, after watching him cook the spiced ground meat in huge, round pans over fires.

Sometimes a grocer she worked for gave her

fruit along with her pay. That was a special treat. And Jasper's nose often found him things to eat on the street.

Each evening, as the sky was getting dark, she would sit with Jasper in their little space, and she would tell him about the sea until they were both ready to sleep. She was lonely, but she was usually too tired to spend much time thinking about it.

One night, Shauzia was jolted out of her sleep by the sound of Jasper barking. She opened her eyes to see lights shining brightly down into her face.

She tried to sit up, but Jasper was standing right on top of her, barking and snarling.

She could feel something grabbing at her, and she tried to pull away. Men's angry voices reached her ears through Jasper's barking. Every time they tried to get hold of her, they were kept back by his snapping jaws and pointed teeth.

"We'll come back with a gun and kill your dog," the men said. "You wait here for us."

They laughed and then went away. Jasper sniffed at Shauzia, licked her face, then lay down right across her belly.

Shauzia clung to Jasper and struggled to breathe through her panic.

"We have to get out of here," she said, gently nudging him to the ground.

They headed off down the alley. Shauzia was shaking so badly that she could hardly walk, and she clung to Jasper's fur for support.

They kept walking for the rest of that night, and avoided all the people they saw.

FIVE

Shauzia and Jasper walked until the sky got light. Exhausted, they collapsed in the doorway of a gun shop on the modern main street of the Saddar Bazaar. They managed to get a bit of sleep until they were chased away by the owner when he came to open his shop for the day.

Shauzia's head was thick with unslept sleep. She kept bumping into people and stumbling over the uneven places on the pavement. Once she walked right into a newspaper stand, almost tipping over the table full of newspapers

"Watch what you're doing!" the angry newspaper seller spat out at her. He kicked Jasper. Jasper yelped at him.

Shauzia pulled her dog away, and they bumped into an Afghan antiques dealer, setting out his goods outside his shop. He yelled at them, too.

"I don't like it here," Shauzia told Jasper,

kneeling to pet him and quiet him down. She pushed her face deep into his soft fur and smelled his good dog smell. The world was full of nasty-tempered adults, and what she really wanted was to never have to see any of them again.

They kept walking. Shauzia just wanted to sit some place and be quiet, but every time they sat down they were told to go away.

She left the main street, wandering through the narrow, dark streets of the older market. Finally she came back into the sunshine where the market ended by the railway tracks.

There were a lot of people here, too, but they were spread out, not so cramped together as they were in the shops. Shauzia felt she could breathe a bit. She and Jasper turned and walked along the tracks.

A small herd of goats and fat-tailed sheep poked their snouts among patches of weeds. Afghan families had set up crude shelters in the dirt beside the tracks. A Pakistani used-clothes pedlar displayed torn Mickey Mouse sweaters and tweed skirts on big sheets of plastic for customers to see. The air smelled of exhaust fumes, excrement and smoke from little cook fires dotted here and there.

A group of Afghan children scavenged in a rubbish heap, dragging large blue sacks behind them. Shauzia watched them for awhile from the tracks. Jasper wagged his tail and strained at his leash, so she let him go. He trotted up to the children, wagging his tail and pushing at them with his snout, wanting to be petted.

Shauzia hung back while the children – four boys and a small girl – greeted Jasper. The little girl was scared at first. Jasper was as tall as she was. But he licked her face, and she giggled, and Shauzia could see she wasn't scared anymore.

"His name is Jasper," she said, leaving the tracks and joining the children. "It's an old Persian name."

"Can he do tricks?" one of the little boys asked.

"Of course he can. He's a very smart dog. Jasper, sit!" Shauzia took him through his tricks. The children left their bags to one side while they played with him, tossing a stick for him to chase and retrieve.

Two of the boys seemed to be around Shauzia's age. The other two were younger, maybe eight or nine years old. Shauzia thought the little girl looked to be around five. She and the smallest of the boys had nothing on their feet. Shauzia wondered how they managed.

She wondered what they were searching for among the garbage, and picked up one of their sacks to take a look.

"That's mine! Are you trying to steal?" One of the older boys pushed her hard away from his bag. Shauzia fell back against the ground, grinding bits of gravel into her palms.

Jasper was beside her in an instant, barking at the boy.

"I wasn't stealing," Shauzia insisted. "I just wanted to see what kinds of things you were collecting." She patted Jasper with long, slow strokes to calm him down.

She got to her feet. Jasper stopped barking. The little girl came up to pet him, and he wagged his tail again.

"You've never picked junk before?" asked the boy who had pushed her.

"Do I look like a junk picker?" Shauzia retorted, brushing herself off. "I work."

"At what?"

"At proper jobs."

"So why don't you go and do your job, and quit trying to steal our stuff?"

Shauzia kicked at the boy's junk bag. "There's nothing in there worth stealing."

"You call this nothing?" He grabbed the bag and pulled out items, waving them under Shauzia's nose.

"Three plastic bottles, a whole newspaper, and two empty tin cans. That's better than you could find!"

"We'll see about that," Shauzia replied.

"This is our junk pile," another boy said. "Why should we share it with you?"

"My dog is a watch dog," Shauzia said. "He'll attack anyone who tries to bother us."

The boy who had pushed Shauzia had bruises on his face, as though he had been in other fights recently.

"Some watch dog," he said. "He doesn't look so fierce." He hung back, though.

"If you're not afraid of him, go ahead and pat him," Shauzia said.

"All right, I will." The boy bent down and reached out a hand. Jasper growled, and the boy backed away.

"It's all right, Jasper," Shauzia said, putting

her hand on the boy's shoulder. "Go ahead and pat him," she said. "Now that he knows you're my friend, he won't hurt you."

The boy held out his hand. Jasper sniffed it, then pushed at the hand with his snout.

"I was sleeping in the alley last night," Shauzia told them. "Some men tried to get at me. Jasper scared them away."

"Would your dog protect us, too?" the little girl asked.

"Sure he would. He'd love to, wouldn't you, Jasper?" Jasper was already wagging his tail so hard he couldn't wag it any harder.

"My name is Zahir," the boy with the bruised face said. The other boys were Azam, Yousef and Gulam, and the little girl's name was Looli.

"I'm Shafiq," Shauzia said, giving them her boy name.

"A boy I know was taken by men like that," Zahir said. "They kept him and they cut something out of his belly before they let him go."

"Was he still alive?" Shauzia asked.

"He was alive for a little while," Zahir replied.

"Then he died," Yousef added.

"Go ahead," Zahir said. "Look in my bag."

Shauzia looked at the collection of cardboard, newspaper, bottles and cans.

"We sell it to a junk dealer," Zahir said.

"Not all of it," Gulam said. "The things that burn, we take home to cook our meals."

"Do you have families?" Shauzia asked.

"Gulam and Looli live with their uncle's family," Yousef said. "The rest of us are on our own."

"So am I," Shauzia said. "How much money do you make?"

"Maybe five roupees. Maybe ten. You can come with us if you like," Zahir said.

The children drifted back to work. Shauzia realized how lucky she'd been to find the jobs she had. She joined them as they sifted through the junk that other people had thrown away.

She started off rooting through the garbage with her foot.

"Not that way," Looli said. She was munching on some dry cones an ice-cream shop had thrown away. "You have to use your hands." She showed Shauzia how to dig right into the pile of garbage to get at whatever might be buried there.

The trash smelled bad, but the smell didn't bother Shauzia. After all, she had lived with sheep for months. The flies were familiar, too. She dug right into the trash, opening plastic bags and dumping the contents onto the ground. She put the paper and rags she found into the little girl's bag.

She would go back to looking for proper jobs tomorrow, she decided, but for today, she just wanted to stay with other children.

Jasper, with his superb dog nose, was good at sniffing out things to eat in the garbage, but Shauzia didn't do too badly, either. Along with the paper and bits of wood from a broken crate, she found an empty spice jar and a cracker box – with some crackers still in it!

"Hey! I found some food!" she exclaimed.

In the next second, she was flat on her back in the trash.

"All food comes to me," Zahir said, holding the box of cracker bits high in the air.

But Shauzia was hungry, and she was tired of being bullied. She sprang up without thinking and threw herself at the boy. They rolled in the trash, trying to hit each other. Jasper jumped around them, barking. The other children picked the spilled cracker bits off the ground and ate them.

Shauzia and Zahir ran out of fight before there was a clear winner. They sat in the trash, brushed themselves off and glared at each other.

"Don't try taking anything away from me again," Shauzia snarled.

"Just remember who's boss here," Zahir snarled back.

Since the crackers were gone anyway, they called a truce and went back to sorting through the junk pile.

Late in the afternoon, one of the smaller boys found a length of string. He tied it to the handle of a plastic shopping bag and ran through the dump along the wasteland beside the railway tracks. The bag fluttered behind him like a bird, high above the garbage and the people making their homes in the dirt.

To Shauzia, it looked beautiful.

The sun was hanging low in the sky when Looli put her tiny arms around Jasper's neck and gave him a hug.

"We have to go now," she said.

Shauzia watched the little girl take her brother's hand as he slung her junk bag and his own over his shoulder, and the two of them walked away.

The other boys shouldered their junk bags and started walking in another direction.

"Are you coming? Zahir called back. "Or do you have some important job to go to?"

The other boys laughed. Shauzia thought about being offended, but decided not to be. She looked at Jasper, shrugged and jogged to catch up to the boys.

For the first part of the evening, they roamed around Peshawar like a pack of animals, tossing odd bits of junk into their bags. "Give us money!" they yelled at everyone they met, laughing when the people looked scared and ran away. Shauzia hung back a little, not yelling, but still very glad to have the company.

By nightfall they had reached a large modern hotel. It was so beautiful, it took Shauzia's breath away.

"Is that a palace?" she asked. She and the boys were scrunched down among some bushes. Across the street a huge white building gleamed in the spotlights. Cars drove slowly up a long driveway lined with large round flower pots overflowing with color. A man in a splendid uniform guarded the double set of doors at the front.

"It's a hotel," Zahir said. "Don't you know what a hotel is?"

"Of course I do," Shauzia lied. There hadn't been such places in Afghanistan. "What are we doing here?" The gravel she was kneeling on pressed into her flesh.

"See the light in the hall?" Zahir pointed to a long, low building that jutted out the side of the hotel. "That means there's a big party tonight."

"I still don't understand."

Zahir sighed at her stupidity.

"We're here for the leftovers. Aren't you hungry?"

Leaving their junk bags hidden among the trees, they scurried around to the back of the hotel. Shauzia heard metal and glass banging and water running. She smelled cooking smells from the open door of the kitchen. Her stomach lurched with hunger.

In a little while, the kitchen staff brought bins out through the back door. They carried the bins over to the back fence and piled rocks on top of them.

"Why are they doing that?" Shauzia asked.

"To keep us out of them. But we're smarter than they are."

The kitchen workers went back inside. Shauzia and the boys crept over to the bins. Shauzia limped a bit, her leg sore from kneeling on the pebbles. Jasper was right in the middle of the children, but he was clever enough to keep quiet.

The boys silently lifted the rocks off the lids of the trash bins. Shauzia helped. They gently tipped over the bins. Then they tore through the party leftovers, tossing aside the balled-up paper napkins and other garbage to get to the cold rice and chicken bones with bits of meat sticking to them.

Shauzia stripped the meat from the bones for Jasper, since chicken bones were bad for him. His nose found him lots of other things to eat, too.

She could not stuff food in her mouth fast enough. Chunks of mutton gristle, bits of ground-meat patties, potatoes slick with spiced oil – she shoveled it all into her mouth, eating with one hand while the other spread out the trash, searching for more food. When a cigarette butt got mixed up with a handful of rice and spinach, she separated it from the food with her teeth, spat it out and kept on eating.

All around her was the sound of hungry boys chewing.

"Hey! Get away from there, or we'll call the police!"

The kitchen workers yelled at the children from the back door.

Shauzia started to leave, but the other kids shouted right back. They heaved bones and other garbage at the workers. Jasper barked, and trash flew through the air. Shauzia picked up a handful of old food and joined in. She laughed as the kitchen workers raised their hands to protect themselves from the flying leftovers.

It felt great to be shouting and throwing. Shauzia couldn't remember when she had last yelled like that. She couldn't raise her voice when she was a shepherd because it would have scared the stupid sheep. She couldn't yell in Kabul because it would have been foolish to draw attention to herself – she didn't need the

Taliban looking closely enough at her to be able to tell she was a girl.

But she could yell here, and she did, and she had a wonderful time.

The men disappeared for a moment, then came back waving frying pans and pot lids. Shauzia saw security guards heading their way, too, their guns drawn.

The children scattered, and they were away from the area before the grown-ups could reach them. When things were quiet again, they retrieved their bags of junk and went looking for a place to sleep.

Shauzia stayed with the boys that night. They slept, huddled together, in a smelly stairwell. Jasper was their watchdog, and he kept them safe.

SIX

Shauzia stood in the aisle of the rich people's grocery store. She ran her finger lightly along the rows of beautiful packages. The pictures on them promised good things inside. Cakes, biscuits with chocolate on top, meat, cheese – food more wonderful than she had ever seen before.

And there was so much of it! Who could possibly mind if she took a few packages for herself and her dog? They had so many!

Her mouth filled with saliva as her fingers curled around a tin with a picture of a fish on the outside. It could so easily move from the shelf to her bag.

"You again!"

A strong hand gripped her shoulder like a claw. She released the tin of fish and was pushed through the shop.

"This is the fourth time today I've had to kick you out. If you come in here again, I will call the police."

The store clerk shoved Shauzia out the door with such force that she hit the pavement at the same moment that the ferocious Peshawar heat hit her. The store had been so lovely and cool, like being surrounded by snow.

She picked herself up off the ground, too angry to pay much attention to the raw skin on her hands and ankles. She stood as close as she dared to the door of the fancy store. At least she could catch a blast of refreshing coldness when the rich people went in and out.

Jasper was stretched out in the bit of shade at the side of the store. He was so hot he had barely managed to growl when she was tossed out.

Shauzia couldn't stand in the shade because she would be out of the way of the people she wanted to beg from.

"Spare any roupees?" she asked a man coming out of the shop. He walked right by her outstretched hand. The woman who came out a short time after handed her a rumpled two-roupee note. That made six roupees Shauzia had made all day.

"I hate this," she said to Jasper. "I hate having to be nice to these people who aren't nice to me. I hate having to ask them for anything. The next person who comes by, I'm going to grab their money and run. If they won't give it to me, I'll just take it."

Jasper rolled his eyes, unimpressed. He had heard this speech before.

Inside the store, Shauzia had felt dizzy at the sight of all the pretty packages of food lined up on the shelves. The people who shopped there had to have a lot of money. Surely people with a lot of money wouldn't mind giving her a bit of it.

But rich people weren't any more generous than poor people.

She asked people for a job as well as for money, but no one had a job for her. She would rather be working than begging. Begging made her feel small.

A man and a woman in Western clothes got out of a white van with their two small boys and crossed the parking lot, heading for the grocery store. Shauzia saw them and held out her hand.

"Look at the dog!" The two boys ran over to Jasper. In an instant he was on his feet, wagging his tail.

"Careful, boys. You don't know this dog," the man said.

Shauzia recognized the language they spoke as English, and she dredged up the English words she knew from when she had studied it in school.

"His name is Jasper," she said.

The man and woman tried to get their sons into the store.

"I need work," Shauzia said. She held out her hand for money, in case they preferred to give her that.

"You speak English very well," the woman said slowly. Then she put a ten-roupee note in Shauzia's hand. "Come, boys, let's go inside."

That's more like it, Shauzia thought, putting the money in her pocket. When the family came out again, the little boys headed straight for Jasper.

"Can we take him home with us, Mommy?" one of the boys asked.

"He belongs to this boy," the woman said. The boy stuck out his lower lip and held Jasper so tightly that Jasper had to shake the boy away.

The man gave Shauzia another ten-roupee

note. "Buy some food for your dog, too," he said. Then the family piled back into the van and drove away.

Shauzia and Jasper stayed outside the grocery store for the rest of the day, but they earned only a few more roupees. She bought some meat patties to share with Jasper, and some nan. Then she went to meet the other boys.

They were using the old Christian cemetery as a camping place. It was shady and cool during the day, and the weeds were soft to sleep on at night. The gravestones all seemed to mark the graves of British soldiers who had died killing Indians. Shauzia didn't know which war that was. She didn't suppose it mattered.

"How did you do today?" Zahir asked. Shauzia held up the bundle of nan. She didn't say how much money she'd made.

One of the boys had some oranges he'd stolen off an old man's karachi. They ate together. Zahir commanded extra food from some of the children, but he didn't bother Shauzia.

"Hello, can I join you?" A small boy, his blue junk bag at his feet, stood on the other side of the graveyard fence.

"Sure. Come on over." Zahir went over to him.

Shauzia knew what was coming.

"Swing your bag up first," Zahir suggested. "It will be easier for you to climb over."

The small boy swung his junk bag up into Zahir's waiting arms. Zahir waited until the boy was almost at the top of the fence, then pushed him hard back onto the sidewalk. The boy tried a few more times before he realized that his junk was gone, and there was nothing he could do about it.

Shauzia didn't join in the scramble for the stolen junk, but she didn't do anything to help the boy, either. She wasn't afraid to fight Zahir, but the last thing she needed was someone depending on her, expecting things from her. She would never get to the sea that way.

"I look after myself. He can do the same," she whispered to Jasper as they settled down among the crosses and tombstones and went to sleep.

Each morning, Shauzia would leave the graveyard, sometimes taking Jasper but usually leaving him in the shade with a pan of water poured from a tap outside the old church nearby. She would walk to the Saddar Bazaar or hitch a ride to other parts of the city to look for work.

Moving around Peshawar so much, she quickly got to know the city. She knew in which neighborhoods she'd most likely find work, which shops gave food away to beggars at the end of the day, and which rich hotels had garbage bins that could be broken into. She learned where there were outdoor water taps, where she could wash a bit and get something to drink. She learned which parks she could nap in during the heat of the day, and which parks had guards who would kick her out before she even got comfortable.

If she was lucky, she worked. If not, she begged. Bit by bit, she kept adding to the roupees in her money pouch.

"We're getting closer to the sea," she told Jasper one evening when they were alone in the graveyard. She showed him the bundle of money. He sniffed at it and wagged his tail. She put the money back in the pouch and hid it under her shirt before any of the boys could return and see it.

"We don't know these boys," Shauzia told Jasper. "All we know is that they're hungry, and you can't trust hungry people. If they knew I had money, they'd steal it from me, just the way I'd steal from them. Well, probably I would."

Boys drifted in and out of the group. Shauzia didn't always learn their names. No one ever said much about themselves. Some things were too hard to talk about

"Can you spare any roupees?"

By now, Shauzia could ask that question in Dari, Pashtu, Urdu, the Pakistani language and English.

"As much as I hate begging, it's worth coming here every Sunday," she told Jasper.

"Here" was the Chief Burger restaurant on Jamrud Road, near University Town, where most of the foreigners lived. People who wanted food stood out on the street and called their food orders through the windows. After they placed their order, they had nothing to do but watch Jasper do his tricks.

The man who ran the burger stand liked Jasper. He gave him water and bits of ground meat. "I'll make the burgers smaller today. If the customers notice, it will be too late. I'll already have their money!"

Shauzia was happy that her dog was eating. She would have liked some meat herself, but she didn't ask, and it was never offered.

She didn't know whether it was the church, or the pizza, or Jasper's tricks, but she always made a lot of money on Sundays. Sometimes she made more than she did when she was working.

There were many regular customers at the Chief Burger. Shauzia remembered them from week to week, and they remembered her – or, at least, they remembered Jasper, since that was who they greeted first.

Shauzia always hoped they would give her a piece of pizza along with their roupees, but they never did. Not even the people she saw often, like the couple in the white van that she had first met outside the grocery store. Their two little boys cried when they had to stop playing with Jasper and go home.

"Spare any roupees?" she called out.

"Would you like some money?" a man asked, coming up beside her.

Adults ask such stupid questions, Shauzia thought.

"Yes, I need money," she replied politely, holding out her hand. "I am also looking for work."

The man handed her a hundred-roupee note.

Shauzia thought her eyes would fall out of her head. She had never held such a beautiful thing before.

"Come with me," the man said. "I will give you a job and then I will give you even more money."

"Oh, thank you," said Shauzia. "I will work very hard for you. Come on, Jasper." She bent down to pick up Jasper's leash.

"Leave the dog," the man said. He took hold of Shauzia's arm.

Jasper growled.

Shauzia tried to bend down to reassure him, but the man tightened his grip and began to pull her along the sidewalk toward his car.

"Wait!" she said. "Just let me see to my dog."

The man did not stop. He held her more tightly.

"You're hurting me!" Shauzia cried. Jasper, hearing the panic in her voice, started to bark at the man. But he kept pulling at Shauzia.

"No!" She tried to pull away. "I don't want to go with you!"

A crowd began to gather. The crowd attracted the police.

"What's happening here?" a policeman asked.

"This boy stole from me, one hundred roupees," the man said.

"I didn't steal! He gave me the money!" Shauzia yelled. "He tried to put me in his car, but I didn't want to go."

"Search him," the man said. "You will find my hundred-roupee note in his pocket."

Shauzia didn't want them searching her and taking the rest of her money. She took the bill out of her pocket and held it out to the man.

"Take it back."

One of the policemen took it.

"Evidence," he said.

Then they grabbed hold of her. Jasper barked madly and threw himself at the policemen.

Shauzia screamed and tried to fight back,

but the police were bigger, and they threw her into the back of their van.

She looked out of the tiny window of the back door of the van in time to see one of the policemen kick Jasper hard. Then the van pulled away, and she could see nothing more.

SEVEN

"Empty your pockets." The guard at the police station pointed at the counter top. Shauzia looked around at the others in the room. They were all men, sitting behind big desks, drinking soft drinks and watching her while fans whirred overhead. No one moved to rescue her. She was the only child in the room, and she felt very, very small.

"I didn't do anything wrong!" She had been insisting that ever since the police threw her in the van.

"Empty your pockets!" the guard insisted. "Empty them, or we will empty them for you."

With shaking hands, Shauzia took the few roupees she'd earned begging that day out of her pocket and put them on the counter.

The guard unfolded her magazine picture of the lavender field. He looked at it, passed it around, then folded it back up.

"You can keep this," he said. Then he noticed the string around her neck. "What are you wearing?"

Shauzia pretended not to know what he was talking about, but it didn't work. He reached out and pulled up her money pouch, taking it right off her neck. He opened it up and dumped the money on the counter in front of him.

Shauzia stared at all her roupee notes, the ones she had worked so hard to earn, the ones that were going to take her to the sea.

With a sweep of the guard's hand, they disappeared into a drawer.

"That's mine!" she shouted.

"What's yours?"

"The money you took. It's mine!"

"What would a boy like you be doing with so much money? You must be a thief!"

Shauzia tried to leap over the counter to get at her money, but the counter was too high, and the policemen were too big. They picked her up, and in the next instant, she found herself being tossed into a cell.

She landed on something soft, then sprang right back to her feet. She grabbed hold of the cell bars and tried to squeeze through them.

"You can't keep my money!" she yelled. "I earned it! It's mine!"

One of the guards banged his stick against the bars, inches from her clenched fists. Shauzia backed away.

"Quiet down, or nobody gets any supper."

"I want my money!" she yelled at the guard's back as he walked away.

"Stop yelling. You'll only make them angry," a voice behind her said.

Shauzia turned around. The cell was full of boys. Most looked a little older. Some were around her age or a little younger. They were sitting on the floor, staring up at her.

"Well, they made me angry," Shauzia replied, kicking at the bars. "What do I care if they're angry."

"Because they'll take it out on all of us."

"So sit down and shut up, or we'll shut you up."

Shauzia sank to the floor. The other boys had to shift around to make room for her.

"I'm going to get my money back," she said quietly. She hugged her knees to stop trembling and scowled to keep from crying.

"Do you have any proof they took your

money?" one boy asked.

"Do you have proof you even had money?" another asked.

"I'll get it back," she repeated. Some of the boys just laughed.

They don't know me, she thought. They laugh because they don't know how determined I am.

Shauzia's panic and rage gave way to discomfort as the afternoon wore on. It was impossible to get comfortable in the cell. The air was hot and didn't move. She longed to lie down or lean her back against something, or stretch her legs out in front of her. There were too many boys on the cement floor of the cell.

Soon her legs were cramped and her back was sore.

The cell stank of unwashed bodies and other foulness. Shauzia found it hard to breathe, and she wondered how the other boys were managing.

Maybe they've been in here so long they've gotten used to it, she thought, just like I got used to the sheep.

She hoped she wouldn't be in the cell that long.

For the first few hours, she jumped at every

little noise that came from outside the cell – every time the phone rang in the outer office, every time one of the guards walked past.

"Relax," one of the older boys said. "You're not going anywhere."

"How do you know?"

"Once you're in here, you're in here forever," he replied. "I was only six years old when they locked me up. Look at me now – old enough to grow a beard soon." The other boys laughed.

Shauzia thought they were probably just joking. The shepherds had joked like that. They made fun of how clumsy she was with chores, or laughed at how one sheep liked to butt her in the behind with his head.

Shauzia hadn't minded. There wasn't much else to laugh at. She concentrated now on not letting her fear show on her face. Anger was good. Fear was dangerous.

"If your family can bring in some money, the police might let you go," the boy next to her said in a quiet voice. "You won't be here forever. Don't listen to them."

"What do I care? I've been in jail lots of times."

"You don't look old enough to have done anything lots of times," an older boy said, and they laughed again.

"How long have you been here?" she asked the boy next to her.

He shifted around a little and pointed to a group of scratches on the wall.

"These are my marks, one for every night." His was only one group of scratches. There were other groups, all over the walls.

Shauzia counted the marks. He had been there almost three months. She didn't let on that she could count.

"I have no family," the boy said, looking ashamed. "Not here. They are back in Afghanistan. I came to earn money to get them out, but now I am in jail. The policeman asks me, 'Where are your papers?' I have no papers. My house was bombed. How could I have papers? So I just sit here."

"Are you telling that same story again?" an older boy complained. "How many times do we have to hear it? Our luck is as bad as yours."

In a lower voice, the boy beside Shauzia continued. "We are all Afghans in this cell. The

Pakistan boys are kept somewhere else. Is your family with you in Peshawar?"

Shauzia couldn't answer. She was trying too hard not to cry.

She had suddenly realized that whenever the phone rang in the office, it would not be for her. There was no one to pay off the police, no one even to know she was there.

She imagined herself making scratches in the wall – endless scratches that would take up the whole wall, blotting out all the other scratches.

How could she stay in this cramped space, with no way to run, no way to get to the sea? She had been outside too long, moving as she pleased. The ceiling pressed down on her. How could she stay here?

It was too unbearable to think about. She thought about Jasper instead. Worrying about her dog was easier than worrying about herself.

"Is there a toilet?" she asked awhile later.

"Can't you smell it?" A boy jerked his thumb to a partitioned-off area at the back of the cell.

Shauzia stepped through boys as if she were stepping through a flower garden. The partition gave her a small amount of privacy, but the toilet was just a stinking hole in the floor.

Sheep are cleaner, she thought, and she did not linger there.

A guard came by with a tray of metal cups of tea and a stack of nan.

"Here is your supper," he said.

The boys dove at the food like the wild dogs Shauzia had seen in Kabul, pushing each other to get to the bread. The guard laughed.

Shauzia ignored the food. The cell door was still being held open by the guard. In an instant, she was on her feet and halfway out of the cell.

"Where do you think you're going?" The guard grabbed her.

"I shouldn't be here," Shauzia yelled, trying to pull away. "I've done nothing wrong!"

"Get back in there!" The guard shoved her into the cell. She fell across the tea tray, spilling the cups that hadn't been snatched up yet. The cell door banged shut.

One of the boys punched her hard in her side. "That was my tea you spilled," he snarled, "and my buddy's tea. You'll have to give us your tea from now on to make up for it."

"I don't have to give you anything," Shauzia snarled back.

"Keep it up," the boy said. "You can't hide from me."

Shauzia went back to her space on the floor. There was, of course, no bread left, or tea.

"Here," the boy beside her said. "I'll share my bread with you." He tore his nan in half and held it out to her.

Shauzia knew that if she accepted his kindness, she would have to show kindness in return, and that would make her look weak. So she shrugged away his offering. She'd been hungry before. Right now, that was the least of her worries.

The boy next to her made another notch in the wall with the edge of his metal cup. The other boys were adding notches to their own groups of scratches.

"I'll make one for you," the boy said, putting a scratch on a bare spot on the wall.

Shauzia looked at it once, then turned away.

The guard collected the tea cups, then turned off the overhead light.

"Pleasant dreams, boys," he sneered.

The boys stretched out on the floor as best

they could in the overcrowded cell. Shauzia did the same, then sat upright again as one of the boys began a low rhythmic moaning.

"That's just the Headbanger," she was told. The moaning boy rocked and banged his head into the wall over and over as he moaned. "He's all right when the lights are on, but he doesn't like the dark. He does this every night. You'll get used to it."

"Soon you'll be like him," another boy said, and several boys laughed.

Shauzia watched the Headbanger for awhile, then lay down again. Fleas bit her ankles and neck. She wrapped her blanket shawl around her to keep them from getting at the rest of her, but was soon so hot that she had to take it off again.

The night went on forever. Some of the boys cried out in their sleep, and the fleas kept biting.

Worry and fear would not let her escape into sleep. She tried to tell herself that things would work out. The police would realize they had made a mistake, and they would let her out in the morning.

But she didn't really believe it. People disappeared in Afghan prisons. Maybe it was the same in Pakistan.

It was awful being separated from Jasper, not having him around to protect her, not being able to reach out and feel him breathing beside her.

Would she go crazy in this terrible place? Would she lose her mind, locked away from the sun? She had seen crazy people in Afghanistan. The craziness took over more and more of their minds until there was nothing left of themselves – just craziness on two legs.

She reached out a hand and put it gently on the chest of the boy sleeping next to her. She could feel his heart beating deep within him. She could feel his lungs take in air and breathe it out again.

She closed her eyes and pretended he was Jasper. And finally, she slept.

EIGHT

Breakfast in prison was more bread and tea. Shauzia grabbed her share of bread and drank her cup of tea before the boy who had punched her could take it. But the tea made just a small dent in her thirst.

"That was mine!" the boy growled.

"Wait awhile and I'll piss it back to you," she said.

The others laughed, and this time they were not laughing at Shauzia.

The boy would have come at her, but just then a guard came to the cell door.

"Get ready for the showers," he said.

The other boys leapt to their feet.

"The water is cold, and it will cool us off," a boy beside Shauzia said. "While we're out, they'll hose down the cell and the toilet. Everything will be better. You'll see."

Shauzia was horrified. There would not be

private showers. She could not expose herself as a girl to all these boys.

She was so scared that she could barely think.

The other boys pressed against the bars at the front of the cell, eager to be first into the showers. It was a chance to stretch their legs, and they yelled and pushed and hit out at each other in their excitement. Shauzia let them push her out of the way, until she was alone at the back of the cell. She pressed herself against the cement.

Maybe if she pressed hard enough, she could push herself right through the wall.

There was a bang on the bars as the guard used his stick to make the boys back up.

"Boy who was brought in yesterday, step forward," the guard called out.

"It was me!" the other boys shouted. "I was brought in yesterday!"

Through all of this, Shauzia heard another voice speaking in English, then switching to Dari.

"No, it's not any of these," the voice said. "Is there another boy in there? The one who was arrested at the Chief Burger?

Shauzia leapt forward, shoving her way to the cell door. On the other side of the bars was one of the after-church-pizza Westerners, the father of the two little boys who liked Jasper so much.

The man smiled down at her. "You have a very smart dog."

Shauzia leaned into the bars and motioned for him to crouch down so she could tell him something.

"You have to get me out of here," she pleaded. "It's shower day."

The man looked perplexed, so she pressed her face against the bars.

"I'm a girl!" she whispered.

He looked at her closely, blinked once, then started talking to the guards. They moved away from the cell door. Shauzia couldn't hear what they were saying, but she could see the Western man take out his wallet and exchange arm-waving gestures with the guards while they talked. Her heart sank when she saw him put his wallet back in his pocket, then leapt when he took it out again. They argued some more. Then the man nodded, took some bills out of his wallet and handed them to the guards.

The guards unlocked the cell door, reached in through the throng of boys and pulled Shauzia out. She looked back at the boys in the cell, then wished she hadn't. Even the bully looked small and lost with his face behind bars.

The Westerner took her by the arm and led her toward the police station exit.

"Wait!" she cried. "They have my money!"

He kept shepherding her through the station. "Your money is gone. It never existed," he said quietly. "Let's just get out of here before they change their minds."

Shauzia's anger bounced around inside her, with no way to get out. But she forgot about it as soon as she walked out of the police station compound, and a large, furry creature threw itself at her so hard she almost fell over.

"Jasper!"

He licked her face all over, and she would have happily sat on the pavement for hours hugging him, if the man hadn't bustled them both into his van.

Shauzia and Jasper stuck their heads out the window and let the breeze rush past them as the van wove in and out of the crazy Peshawar traffic. The fresh air felt wonderful, even filled with heat and exhaust fumes.

"What's your name?" the man asked.

"My girl name is Shauzia. My boy name is Shafiq," Shauzia said, pulling her head in. She laughed at the way Jasper looked, fur flying back from his face.

"My name is Tom."

"How did you find me?"

He handed her a plastic bottle of water, and she drank deeply while he told her.

"It was your dog," he said. "When we got to the Chief Burger for our pizza yesterday, Jasper practically threw himself at us. We asked around and found out what had happened. I'm sorry it took so long, but it took all this time to find you and persuade the police to let you go."

"Where are we going now?"

"Barbara, my wife, made me promise to bring you home if I was able to get you out of jail. She'll be delighted that you're a girl. Why are you pretending to be a boy?"

"I just felt like it," she lied, keeping her privacy out of habit more than a distrust of Tom.

"Is your family still back in Afghanistan?" he asked.

"They're dead," she lied again, then stuck her head back out the window. She couldn't remember the last time she had ridden in such a fast-moving vehicle.

If I had one of these, she thought, I could be at the sea in no time.

They turned into University Town, a neighborhood of big trees, high walls and flowered shrubs spilling their blossoms into the street. The noise of the traffic on Jamrud Road was left behind as the van made several turns, finally stopping before a high metal gate in a wall.

Tom got out, unlocked and opened the gate, then drove the van through.

Shauzia and Jasper stepped out of the van into a whole new world.

"Daddy's home! Daddy's home!" The two small boys rushed along the front porch and ran through the garden to hug their father. Behind them, wiping her hands on a dishcloth, came their mother, Barbara. She put her hands on Shauzia's shoulders.

"So Tom was able to get you out! Welcome to our home."

Shauzia looked up into Barbara's face. Her

smile was warm. Shauzia couldn't remember anyone smiling at her like that before, except Parvana.

"You must be hungry," Barbara said. "We have lots of food in the house to feed a hungry boy."

"The hungry boy is a hungry girl," Tom said, swinging his small giggling son in a circle.

Barbara looked down at Shauzia. "A girl! Oh, how wonderful! I'll have some company in this house full of boys. Come inside. We'll get you cleaned up and fed, and you can tell us all about yourself."

Shauzia's eyes almost burned from the bright colors of all the flowers in the courtyard garden. Birds were singing in the trees. The rest of Peshawar, beyond the high walls, might not even have existed.

Her eyes grew wide when Barbara drew her into the house. The entranceway alone was bigger than the room she had shared with her whole family back in Kabul.

"Tom is an engineer," Barbara said as she took Shauzia from room to room. "He builds bridges, mostly in the northern part of Pakistan. We're here on a two-year contract.

Our families thought we were nuts to come, especially with the children, but we like a bit of adventure. We're from Toledo, in the United States. There's not much adventure there."

Shauzia was glad of Barbara's chatter. She felt shy amid so much wealth. The house had a living room with big windows that looked out onto the garden. The chairs looked soft, and there were lots of cushions in pretty colors. A television set was showing cartoon characters singing a bouncy English song. Toys littered the floor.

"Here is our dining room," Barbara said as they passed through a room with a long wooden table surrounded by chairs. Shauzia looked at all the dishes stacked in a glass-windowed cupboard. "And this is our kitchen."

They walked into a large sunny room, the source of the good smells Shauzia had been sniffing since she had walked into the house. Tins of food and fancy boxes of cookies and crackers were stacked neatly on shelves. A bowl overflowed with fruit.

Shauzia just wanted to look at everything and smell the good smells, but Barbara kept her moving.

They went upstairs, where there were more

rooms and more toys on the floor. Children's clothes were scattered everywhere.

"Please excuse the mess," Barbara said, as Shauzia stepped over a toy truck. "I'm trying to teach the boys to clean up after themselves, but they simply refuse to cooperate." Then she showed Shauzia a lovely blue room with a pattern of little flowers on the wall. There was a Western toilet, gleaming taps and a shower stall with a blue curtain.

My family lived like this once, Shauzia thought, a long, long time ago, before the bombs started falling. The memory of it seemed like another person's life, not her own.

"Into the shower with you," Barbara said. She showed Shauzia how to work the taps. "Use as much soap as you want. Leave your dirty clothes on the floor. I'll find you something clean to wear."

Then she left her alone.

Shauzia was glad for some time to catch her breath. She gently touched her finger to the blue-flowered wallpaper, then felt the smoothness of the tile.

There was a mirror over the sink. She walked over and looked into it.

She didn't recognize the head that stared back at her. It had been years since she had seen her face. The room she had shared with her family in Kabul had no mirror.

In her mind, she was still a schoolgirl in a uniform with long dark hair that curled up at the end. But the face that looked back at her now was older than she remembered. It was longer and the cheeks were hollower. Shauzia wondered who this girl was.

There were noises downstairs as the boys came back into the house. Shauzia heard Jasper's feet running up the stone staircase and whimpering outside the bathroom door. She left her reflection and let him in.

"You don't care what I look like, do you, Jasper?" His wagging tail made her feel better.

She shucked her filthy clothes and got into the shower. She turned on the taps and let the hot water stream over her body. The soap smelled of flowers and spices. She lathered and rinsed, lathered and rinsed, washing the grime and stink off her body.

"Why don't you join the children in the garden?" Barbara suggested when Shauzia appeared in the kitchen dressed in a woman's shalwar kameez. It felt great to be clean and dressed in clean clothes. Her skin smelled good, like the soap. Barbara handed her a glass of cold milk. "Dinner will be ready soon."

Shauzia and Jasper went into the garden where the boys were playing. One boy had a truck the other boy wanted, and they started to argue. Shauzia didn't like to look at them. They were chubby with good health, and their laughter and arguing hurt her ears.

She tasted the milk. It was smooth and good. She poured some into the palm of her hand and held it out to Jasper.

"Let me do that!" one of the boys yelled, and they both crowded in on her, eager and demanding. Shauzia leaned back to get away from them, but they kept pressing in on her.

She was rescued by Tom, who called them all in to supper.

"Shauzia, you sit here." Barbara pulled out a chair for her at the long wooden table. In front of her was a bright yellow plate and shining cutlery. On the table were platters of chicken and bowls of vegetables. Barbara poured her another glass of milk while Tom supervised the boys as they washed their hands.

"Have you used a fork before?" Barbara asked.

Shauzia nodded. Many Afghans ate with their fingers, but her family had been very modern. They had lost all their cutlery in a bombing and ate with their fingers after that, but Shauzia still remembered how to eat with a fork.

She watched Tom and Barbara put napkins on their laps, and she did the same.

Once she started eating, she didn't think she could stop. At first she tried to copy the adults and use her fork properly, but that was too slow, so she used her fingers, too. She ignored everything except the food. Barbara kept refilling her plate, and Shauzia ate it all, without really distinguishing between chicken, rice or vegetables.

When she started to get full, she remembered to save some food for the next day. The napkin came in handy for that.

"Do you still have room for dessert?" Barbara asked, placing a bowl of chocolate ice cream in front of her.

"I want ice cream!" the smaller boy, Jake, whined.

"Eat your carrots first," Barbara said.

"No!"

"Eat just one bite of carrot," Tom said.

Shauzia watched as Jake, frowning, put the tiniest piece of carrot into his mouth. Barbara took his plate away and replaced it with ice cream. Shauzia eyed the food that was still on the plate as Barbara carried it to the kitchen, then turned her attention to her ice cream.

It was so good, she picked up her bowl and licked up the remains of it.

"Paul, put your bowl down," Tom said to the older boy.

"But she got to!"

"Never mind. You know better."

Shauzia felt her cheeks burn. She had made a mistake. Would they throw her out?

"I've made up a bed for you in the spare room," Barbara said. "Do you want to see it now? Then you can go to sleep any time you want to."

Shauzia nodded and got up from the table, holding her napkin full of food down by her side.

"Jasper's sleeping with me tonight," Jake announced.

"No, he's not. He's sleeping with me," insisted Paul.

Shauzia left them to their argument. Jasper trotted along beside her as they went upstairs.

After brushing her teeth with a new red toothbrush, she saw her bedroom. It had a real bed in it, with sheets and blankets and a pillow. Barbara handed her a nightgown to put on. She was suddenly very tired.

Barbara gave her a hug. "Sleep well. We're very glad to have you here."

Shauzia's arms remained at her side. She wasn't sure if she should return the hug. She wasn't sure if she could remember how.

Barbara showed her where to turn off the light, then left her alone.

Shauzia hid the food under the bed. She changed into the nightgown and slid into bed between clean sheets. Her belly was so full it hurt, and her skin still smelled of the soap from the shower.

Jasper hopped up on the bed and stretched out beside her.

"I think they're going to ask us to stay here with them," she whispered. "I could clean for them, and at night, when everyone is asleep, I could play with some of those toys. I could go back to school, and learn to be... anything!"

She leaned on her elbows and looked into Jasper's face. "We'll still go to the sea. We'll still go to France But would it be all right with you if we stayed here for a little while?"

Jasper thumped his tail and licked her hand.

Shauzia put her head back on the very soft pillow. "I wish Mrs. Weera could see me now," she whispered. Then she smiled and fell asleep.

She woke up a few hours later. After listening carefully to make sure everyone was sleeping, she tiptoed downstairs to the kitchen. The garbage was full of perfectly good food. She rescued it, took it upstairs and hid it under her bed.

She could never tell when she would be hungry again.

NINE

The next few days passed by in a haze of eating and sleeping.

Shauzia hadn't realized how tired she was. Inside this walled-in paradise there were birds and flowers and no piles of garbage to search through.

She ate three meals a day at the big table, plus the snacks that Barbara handed out between meals.

"Make yourself at home," she told Shauzia. "We want you to be comfortable."

"Why are you doing this?" Shauzia asked.

"Tom's salary goes a long way over here," Barbara told her. "We like to share what we have. Besides, us girls have to stick together!" She gave Shauzia another hug, and this time, Shauzia hugged her back.

Sometimes beggars would ring the bell outside in the street, and Tom or Barbara would open the door in the gate and hand out oranges or coins. The gate was high and made of thick steel, so Shauzia never saw the people who came to the door, but she was glad they were getting some help.

She kept intending to help out around the house, but she kept dozing off instead. She would sit down for a moment after breakfast or lunch, in the living room or on the porch, and wake up several hours later.

"I'm sorry," she said to Barbara, after sleeping away the afternoon and not helping with dinner.

"You've been tired for a long time," Barbara said, putting her arm around Shauzia's shoulders. "You'll get caught up on your rest soon, and then you'll feel better."

Shauzia liked it when Barbara smiled at her. She liked to watch her and Tom wrestling with their boys, or playing trucks with them, or reading to them at bedtime.

Tom and Barbara spoke Dari to her, but the boys knew only English. Shauzia turned over each new word she heard in her head, and whispered it to Jasper until she felt comfortable saying it out loud. Bit by bit, her English improved.

No one spoke about the future. Shauzia didn't want to ask. Maybe they had forgotten that she was an outsider. Maybe they already thought of her as one of their own children. She didn't want to remind them that she wasn't.

One day, Shauzia woke up in the morning and felt really awake.

"I think I've caught up on my sleep," she said to Jasper. Jasper looked good, too. He'd been eating well, and his coat was soft from lots of washing and brushing.

"You look bright-eyed this morning," Tom said to her at breakfast.

"I'd like to start helping out," Shauzia said, pleased to be noticed. "I'm very good at cleaning."

"We already have a cleaning woman," Jake said, his mouth full of scrambled eggs.

"Waheeda only comes twice a week, which is not enough to keep this place clean," Barbara said. "If you two boys would only pitch in and pick up your toys now and then."

"Talk to the hand," Paul said, stretching his arm, palm out, to his mother.

"You know I don't like that. He got it from a video," Barbara told Shauzia.

"Maybe you shouldn't watch videos for awhile," Tom said. Paul slammed his fork onto the table, scattering bits of egg. He made the loud whining sound that hurt Shauzia's ears.

Shauzia took advantage of the distraction to take more eggs from the platter, and to put them and some toast into her napkin. The pile of food under her bed was getting bigger every day. If Tom and Barbara ever asked her to leave, she'd have food to last for quite awhile. Maybe it would last until she got to the sea.

"I'd like to take the boys swimming this afternoon," Barbara told Shauzia when they were doing the lunch dishes together. "We go to the American Club. I wish I could take you, but it's only for ex-patriots. You know, foreigners? Would you be all right here on your own for a few hours?"

Shauzia found the question funny. After all, she had been looking after herself for a long time

"I will be all right," she said.

She waved goodbye as they drove away and closed the gate after they left.

She was almost back in the house when the gate buzzer rang.

"Don't answer the doorbell," Barbara had said. "I have a key for the gate, so we'll let ourselves in."

Shauzia was going to do as Barbara said, but the buzzer sounded again. She couldn't just leave someone out there.

She opened the door in the gate. An Afghan woman was holding a baby, her hand stretched out.

"Can you give me something for my children?"

"Yes, I can. Come into the garden." Shauzia ran into the house and filled a plastic bag with fruit and biscuits from the cupboard. She handed it to the woman, who thanked her many times, then left.

"That was fun," Shauzia said to Jasper. She went into the house and was just settled on the living-room floor, getting ready to play with the toys, when the bell rang again.

This time it was a group of children carrying junk sacks, looking for cardboard or cans to add to their collections.

Shauzia had an idea.

"Come in," she said. "Come in and play."

She got food for everyone and showed them

the toys. The children looked like they didn't know what to do with them. Shauzia closed a small hand around a toy car and made it move across the floor.

The bell rang a few times more. She brought a heavily pregnant woman into the house and took her up to one of the beds to sleep in a cool, dark room. An old man drank a glass of milk and fell asleep in the shade of the garden.

More women and children came to the door. Shauzia invited everyone in. "The people who live here like to share," she said. Jasper greeted them and made everyone feel welcome.

Shauzia gave out food until the cupboards and the fridge were empty. When there was no more food to give away, she handed out toys, clothes, blankets – anything the beggars could use.

With everyone eating, the children playing with toys and with Jasper, the house felt like it was having a party.

"Here's a pillow for your back," she said to one woman, handing another a pair of Barbara's sandals to replace the ripped ones she had come in with. She took people up to the bathroom so they could shower, and found a supply of bars of soap in a cupboard. She handed these out, too.

Shauzia was up in the bathroom, helping two little girls shower and wash their hair, when Barbara and the boys came home. The girls were giggling so much at the soap bubbles in their hair, Shauzia almost missed Barbara's shriek. Then Barbara shrieked a second time, and Shauzia definitely heard that.

"What is going on here?" Barbara yelled. "Shauzia!"

Shauzia, her hands full of hair she was rinsing, called down to her. "I'm up here."

Barbara was in the bathroom in seconds.

"Look how clean they are," Shauzia said, wrapping the little girls in towels.

"Who are all these people? What have you been doing?"

Shauzia smiled up at her. "Sharing. Like you shared with me."

"Sharing?"

"They came to the gate. They needed things."

"And you just invited them in?"

Shauzia didn't understand. "I thought you

would be pleased. I thought this is what you like to do. You have so much."

"Where are their clothes?" Barbara's face was hard as she looked down at the little girls, dripping water on her bathroom floor.

Shauzia pointed to the sink. She had put the clothes in water to soak before washing them. She was planning to wrap the girls in sheets while the hot Peshawar sun dried their clothes.

Barbara wrung the excess water out of the clothes and handed them to Shauzia.

"Get the girls dressed," she said, and then she went downstairs. Shauzia heard her telling the other people to get out.

"Mommy! There's a lady sleeping on my bed!" Jake hollered, and soon the pregnant woman was out of the house, too.

Shauzia helped the little girls get dressed in the wet clothes, and she ushered them out the gate.

"I'm sorry," she said to them.

"That was fun," one girl said. "We smell good now." Shauzia watched them walk down the lane, dragging their junk bags behind them.

"Look at this mess," Barbara said, picking up the toys and dishes that littered the room.

"I'll help," Shauzia said, bending down to pick up a plate.

Barbara put a hand on her shoulder. "You've done enough. Please go and sit in the garden." There was no warmth in Barbara's voice or face.

Tom came home an hour later. Shauzia stayed outside, but she could still hear their voices, rising and falling.

"No food left in the house! Things missing – toys, clothes. Strangers in our beds!"

In a little while, Tom came out with the boys.

"We're going to get pizza!" Jake said. "Can Jasper and Shauzia come with us?"

"No, we'll be right back," Tom said, and they drove away.

That evening, Shauzia finally got to taste pizza. She liked it very much, but the atmosphere at the table was too tense for her to really enjoy it.

After supper, Shauzia washed the dishes. Barbara and Tom took the boys upstairs to get them settled for the night. Shauzia heard another shriek, this one from one of the boys.

A moment later, Tom called down the stairs. "Shauzia, could you come up here?"

They were all in her room. A swarm of ants was moving on her floor and under her bed.

"Why were you hiding food?"

"So I'd have something to eat when... " She stopped talking.

"When what?"

"When I didn't have anything else to eat."

"I'll get the broom," Tom said after an awkward silence. He swept up the rotten, ant-infested food. Barbara washed the floor. Shauzia stood in a corner, watching them and feeling small.

Breakfast was delayed the next morning while Tom went out to buy groceries. It was the middle of the morning by the time they ate.

"We'd like to get you some new clothes," Barbara said when they were gathered around the table. "We'd like you to have something new to take with you to the refugee camp."

Shauzia put her glass of milk back on the table. She made her face say nothing.

"It's not that we haven't enjoyed having you here," Barbara said, "but we need to just be together as a family."

"I went to see a friend of mine this morning who works for one of the aid agencies," Tom said. "He told me about a special orphans and widows' section of one of the refugee camps. The woman who runs it is used to taking in new children unexpectedly."

"You'll be able to go to school there," Barbara said cheerfully. "Tom's friend says they even have a nurse's training program."

"There are so many Afghan children like you," Tom said. "We can't possibly take care of everyone."

Shauzia straightened her back and raised her chin. She didn't need them to take care of her.

"The children love your dog," Barbara said. "We'd be happy to give him a home here with us. After all, what sort of life will he have in the camp?"

Jasper moved closer to Shauzia and put his paws on her lap.

"Well," said Barbara, stiffly. "Would you like girl clothes or boy clothes?"

"Boy clothes, please," Shauzia replied. She then proceeded to eat everything in sight. Food was food. And she was still a long way from the sea.

She kept her arm around Jasper in the van

all the way to the refugee camp. She could still smell the laundry soap on her clothes. In her lap was a bag with a new boy's shalwar kameez, some candies, a toy car with only two wheels that Jake had given her and a small bar of the good-smelling soap.

Barbara and the boys stayed behind at their house while Tom drove Shauzia back along the road that had first brought her to the city. Tom kept his eyes on the traffic and did not speak to her.

I could push him out of the driver's seat, she thought, picturing Tom bouncing and rolling along the highway. She could take his place behind the wheel and drive the van to the sea. How hard could it be to drive? There were a lot of bad drivers in Peshawar. She'd just be one more.

She didn't do it, though. She didn't push Tom out onto the highway, and she was still in the van when it passed through the main gates of the refugee camp and into its maze of mud-walled streets.

"You'll be fine here," Tom said after stopping the van in front of the entrance to the Widows' Compound. "There are lots of other children here, and I'm told that the woman in charge will be happy to have you."

Shauzia and Jasper got out of the van.

"Would you like me to go in with you?" Tom asked.

Shauzia shook her head. It was right to thank Tom, so she said thank you, and she meant it.

But as she watched his van drive away, she couldn't help thinking that all he'd done was take her out of one prison and put her into another.

"Shauzia's back!" Children streamed out of the compound and threw their arms around her and Jasper. Jasper kissed everyone hello, and wagged his tail so fast it was almost a blur.

Shauzia was surrounded by the stinky camp smell again. She could no longer smell the laundry soap on her clothes, and the flowery scent had already left her skin.

She opened the bag and gave away the candies, the car and the shalwar kameez. She kept the little bar of soap.

She'd use it to give Jasper a bath.

When they got to the sea.

TEN

Rows and rows of purple flowers, fields and fields of them. Sun shining down out of a brilliant blue sky. A place where nothing bad ever happened.

Deep creases lined the picture. It had been folded up in Shauzia's pocket for a long time. The edges were frayed.

"I don't understand, Jasper," Shauzia said. They were sitting by a wall in the shade. "I used to be able to look at this picture and imagine myself there, sitting among the flowers. It was so clear in my head. It looked like a magical place. Now it just looks like a picture torn out of a magazine." She showed it to Jasper. He didn't even raise his head. He'd seen it way too often.

"Maybe you're right," she conceded. "Maybe I should forget it. It will take ages to earn the money, and I just don't know if I can face trying to do it again. The thought of starting over is awful. Besides, what's so great about a field of purple flowers? It's probably full of thorns. And snakes."

She started to tear up the paper. Jasper raised his head and growled low in his throat. So she folded the picture back up instead and put it back in her pocket.

She stared at the mud wall across the alley.

"I can't stay here, though. I can't look at these walls for the rest of my life."

She lay down on the ground so that her head was close to Jasper's. "I'll tell you a secret," she said quietly. "I still want to get to France. I still want to get to the sea. But I just don't want to be alone anymore. What do I do about that?"

Jasper kissed her nose. It was no answer, but she felt better.

No one said anything to Shauzia about her time away. Mrs. Weera must have asked them not to. The little kids hugged her and said they'd missed her, the same way they hugged and said they'd missed Jasper, but no one asked her what had happened and why she was back.

At first she wished someone would, especially one of the boys her age. She felt like fighting someone.

As the days went by, though, the anger drained out of her. She spent most of her time following patches of shade around the compound.

Mrs. Weera was being as annoying as always, but in an entirely new way.

She did not give her any more little jobs.

"You'll be wanting to leave again soon to get to the sea, dear," she said when Shauzia picked up some empty water jugs to get filled at the United Nations water pump outside the compound. "Save your strength for that."

Mrs. Weera took the jugs from Shauzia's hands and called a boy over to fetch the water.

That was two weeks ago. Lazing around while others did all the work was fun for awhile, but now Shauzia was so bored she could hardly stand it.

"Are you still here?" Mrs. Weera asked, striding by Shauzia on her way to another part of the compound. "I thought you'd be long gone by now. An active girl like you must be getting awfully bored just sitting around." She kept walking with those quick, giant steps of hers.

Shauzia leapt to her feet. She wanted to yell something, but she couldn't think of anything to say, so she kicked the wall of the hut instead. Hurting her foot made her angrier, and what made it even worse was that there were two boys nearby who watched the whole thing.

They were playing soccer, using a small rock as a ball, and they paused in their game long enough to laugh at her.

"What are you looking at?" Shauzia yelled at them. "And why are you wasting time with games when there is work to be done around here? See those empty water jugs over there? Go and get them filled. Do what I tell you!"

With each word Shauzia came closer and closer to the boys, until she was yelling right in their faces. She paused to take a breath and they ran off, grabbing the empty jugs on their way to the UN pump.

"That was fun!" Shauzia said to Jasper. She looked around the camp with new eyes. "Mrs. Weera thinks she's so good at running things, but there's a lot around here that's not being done properly. Anything she can do, I can do ten times better. Come on."

She started out, then realized Jasper hadn't moved. He was sitting on his haunches and watching her.

She bent down and scratched his ears. "Don't look at me like that. We are going to the sea. We are going to France, and we'll send Mrs. Weera a letter telling her how happy we are to be away from her. But we'll go when I say, not when Mrs. Weera says we should go. And I just don't feel like going right now."

Shauzia threw herself into activity. Instead of taking orders from Mrs. Weera, she thought up projects on her own.

She organized scrounging parties with the older children. They would go to other parts of the camp and pick up stray boards or bits of pipe and anything else they could find lying around that might be useful.

She started an arithmetic class for the little kids, using stones to teach them how to form their numbers.

"One day you will be working," she told

them. "If you don't know how to count, you won't know if your boss is cheating you."

She fetched the compound's ration of flour and cooking oil from the warehouse and took her turn carrying containers of water from the UN pump. She stayed out of Mrs. Weera's way, and Mrs. Weera left her alone.

She even made a friend. Farzana was a few years younger than Shauzia, and she was new in the compound. She had been living in another part of the camp with her aunt. Mrs. Weera brought her to the Widows' Compound when her aunt died and there was no one else to take care of her.

"She wasn't really my aunt," Farzana told Shauzia. "I had a real aunt, but she died. I get passed from person to person. I'm glad to be here, because there are so many people. I won't have to move again when somebody dies."

Farzana and Shauzia often went together when Shauzia had errands to do outside the compound. She liked having a friend again. It was almost like having Parvana back.

Everything in the camp was on the verge of falling apart, including many people. Every day they saw men and women sitting against the walls that lined the streets, staring into space. Others talked to themselves. Many looked so sad, Shauzia wondered if they would ever be able to smile again.

I have to get out of here, she thought. I don't want to end up like them.

The clay streets and walls held onto the summer heat.

"I feel like a loaf of nan baking in the oven," Farzana said one particularly hot afternoon.

The air wasn't moving. They sat in the coolest spot they could find, as far away from the others as possible, but it wasn't very satisfactory. If they wanted privacy, they had to put up with the stink of the open sewers. If they wanted less stink, they had to put up with more people.

The babies fussed in the heat, and many of the children had sore bellies. The compound was always filled with the sound of crying and whining.

"The sea will be cool," Shauzia said without thinking.

"What's the sea?" Farzana asked.

"The Arabian Sea, by the city of Karachi," Shauzia said. "It flows into the Indian Ocean."

"What's an ocean?" Farzana asked.

Shauzia was stunned. "An ocean is, well, it's water, a lot of water, in one place."

Farzana was quiet for a moment. "There is an ocean in this camp. I'll take you there this evening, after the day cools down. It's in the part of the camp where I used to live with my aunt."

They fell asleep in the shade. If Mrs. Weera was yelling out orders anywhere in the camp, they blissfully didn't hear her

"Here's our ocean," Farzana said later that day. They were standing by a square cement pond, maybe thirty paces long on each side. It was full of water. It was also full of garbage, green scum and sewage. Clouds of mosquitoes and other bugs hovered over it.

Shauzia watched a woman dip a bucket into the slimy mess and haul some water away.

"That's not an ocean," Shauzia said. "An ocean is water as far as a person can see. It's deep and blue and smells good, and I'm going to go there."

"I'd like to see something like that," Farzana said. "Take me with you."

"I can't take you with me to the ocean. It's a very long way, and I'm having enough trouble getting myself there. Besides, I'm not stopping once I get to the sea. I'm going on, and I don't want anyone slowing me down. How could I take you with me?"

Farzana turned her back to Shauzia. "I don't need anyone to take me anywhere. I can get to the sea by myself."

Shauzia watched her walk away. The younger girl's head was held high, but Shauzia knew she'd hurt her feelings.

"Maybe I should say yes," she said to Jasper. "It would be a lie, but it would make her happy for a little while." Sometimes it was hard to know the right thing to do.

Shauzia hurried after her friend.

"All right," she said. "I'll take you with me. We'll go to the sea together."

ELEVEN

Shauzia fanned away the flies that kept collecting on the sweat on her face. All around her, others were doing the same.

"Every time we come here, we wait," a man beside her said. "Do you think we have nothing else to do? I should be looking for a job."

"Are there jobs around here?" Shauzia asked.

"There is work in Peshawar," the man replied.

Shauzia brushed the flies away again and went back to her thoughts. She wasn't ready to return to Peshawar.

She was sitting with hundreds of others in the camp's central warehouse. They were waiting for the flour to be distributed.

"Why don't I just go and get it at the end of the day?" she had asked Mrs. Weera.

"Because by then our allotment could have disappeared. You need to be there to grab our ration when it comes in." The flour was delivered on a big truck by an aid agency.

At the end of the afternoon, one of the warehouse guards announced to the crowd, "No flour today. Go back to your homes."

"What do you mean, no flour?" a man called out. "I can see it through the window. I have children to feed."

"That flour is for other people," the guard said. "There is not enough to give out to you today. Go back to your homes."

There was nothing else to do. Shauzia and the others went back to their homes.

"We can make do without it for a few days," Mrs. Weera said, when Shauzia told her what happened.

"How?" Shauzia demanded. A picture of the full shelves and refrigerator in Tom and Barbara's house came into her head. She pushed it aside. "We should complain to somebody."

"We will manage," Mrs. Weera said, putting an end to the argument. They managed by eating less.

Shauzia went back to the warehouse on the next scheduled day for flour distribution, at the end of the week. The same thing happened again, and Shauzia returned to the Widows' Compound empty handed.

When it happened again the following week, she was fed up. And hungry.

"I should go back to the city," Shauzia grumbled to Mrs. Weera. "I could find a job there and buy something to eat."

"But how would you get the food back here?" Mrs. Weera asked. "You're not thinking, Shauzia."

"Why would I bring the food back here? I'm not responsible for all these people!"

"Yes, you are. And so am I. We have two good legs, two good arms, two good eyes, and minds that work properly. We have a responsibility to those who don't have what we have."

"Then let's do something," Shauzia yelled. "Everyone in the compound is hungry, and we just sit here on our two good legs and do nothing."

"I've already met with the camp management," Mrs. Weera replied. "There's nothing we can do. The aid agency that sends us flour is dependent on donations. If they don't have the money, how can they buy flour?"

"But there's flour in the warehouse, just sitting there. I saw it through the window."

"That flour must be for some other group of people."

"So we just starve?"

"I've put out a call to other women's organizations, and I'm sure they will help us. Until then, we must be patient."

Shauzia stomped away in frustration.

"We hate being patient, don't we, Jasper?" Jasper wagged his tail in agreement.

Shauzia remembered the raids on the hotel garbage cans. She had an idea.

"The guards only watch the front door," she told Farzana. "They don't watch the back window. They're too lazy."

They came up with a plan. They needed the help of a dozen of the older children in the compound. They all said yes. Everyone was hungry.

They left the compound early the next morning, just as the sky was getting light. Jasper went with them. None of the adults saw them leave.

Farzana and one of the small boys went to the front of the storehouse. Their job was to keep the guards occupied by talking to them and asking endless questions. The rest of the children went to the back of the storehouse. Shauzia pried open the window with a knife she had borrowed from the compound's kitchen.

They soon had bags of flour making their way out the window and onto the little wagon they had brought with them.

Shauzia never knew how word of what they were doing got out. She didn't recall seeing anyone on their way to the warehouse, but there were a lot of people in the camp with nothing to do but watch other people.

The children's wagon was only half filled with sacks of flour when the first adults started to show up. The larger men pushed the children out of the way and tried to snatch the flour off their wagon. Children had to drape themselves over the sacks of flour to protect them.

The noise the adults made brought the guards, and the noise the guards made brought more people out to the warehouse.

In what seemed to be only moments, a large crowd had gathered. Everyone pushed to the window and tried to break down the front doors to get at the flour. A crowd always draws a bigger crowd, and there was soon a full-fledged riot.

A huge mob of hungry, desperate people swarmed around the storehouse. Shauzia was in a panic about Farzana and the small boy with her, but she couldn't get to them. The crowd of grown-ups was too thick, too crazy with hunger and anger.

There was too much yelling, too much pushing. People beat against the storehouse with sticks, and when they couldn't reach the warehouse, they beat on each other.

Shauzia still had a bag of flour clutched tightly in her arms. She used it to protect her as she pushed toward the crowd.

Someone started pulling on it. Shauzia looked up. A man twice her size was trying to grab her flour.

"I have hungry children to feed!" he yelled.

"What do you think I am?" Shauzia yelled back.

He was bigger and stronger. He raised his arm and slammed his fist into Shauzia's head. She dropped to the ground. Her head hit the dirt with a thud, and she watched the man run off with her flour.

She wanted to get up off the ground and run after him. She wanted to hit him the same way he had hit her, and grab back the flour that she needed to feed herself and her friends. But that message was not making the journey from her brain to her body. All she could do was lie on the ground and watch the legs of the rioters run around and around.

Many of the flour bags broke in the struggle. The ground around Shauzia soon looked like Kabul in the winter, as the flour swirled in the air and settled on the dirt.

The rioters paid no attention to Shauzia. Her body rolled this way and that as people rushed around her and over her, often stepping right on her as if she was a log, rather than a person.

Someone big and heavy stepped on her leg. Shauzia felt a snap. She cried out in pain. Her cries were lost among the yelling of the rioters.

Another blow landed on her head, and then everything went black.

She was unconscious when Jasper finally found her. He stood over her, barking furiously at everyone who came close, protecting her from the raging crowd.

TWELVE

Shauzia's head felt like it was buried under a load of rocks. The noises around her were unfamiliar, and she struggled to open her eyes. The best she could do was open one eye a teeny bit, but not enough to see through. The effort was too much for her, and she dropped into darkness once again.

Some time later, she was able to stay awake long enough to make a sound. Her chest and her head hurt terribly, and what was the matter with her leg? She opened her mouth just wide enough to moan. Then she passed out.

"Shauzia."

Shauzia heard someone calling for her at the end of a long, long tunnel.

"Shauzia."

Bit by bit, the tunnel grew shorter.

"All right, Shauzia. It's time to wake up."

Something was familiar about the voice, but

Shauzia's brain was working too slowly to be able to pinpoint what it was.

"Shauzia! Wake up! No more nonsense!"

That did the trick. Some of the darkness lifted from Shauzia's brain. She managed to open one eye long enough to see Mrs. Weera's face hovering over her.

"What... "

"You're in the clinic," Mrs. Weera said. "You've been banged up a bit, but nothing to be frightened of. You'll soon be back in the game."

Mrs. Weera's brash cheerfulness was hard on Shauzia's ears. She waved her arm slightly, telling Mrs. Weera to go.

"No, no need to thank me," Mrs. Weera said, taking hold of Shauzia's hand and putting it between her two strong ones. For a moment Shauzia felt safer than she had ever felt before.

Then Mrs. Weera spoke again.

"And I know you're sorry for causing so much trouble. We'll take care of all that later. Right now, just rest and recover. We'll have you back in shape before you know it."

Shauzia felt the bed shift as Mrs. Weera stood up. She closed her eye. She was glad Mrs. Weera was keeping her visit short.

"Since you have Shauzia for a while, why not get her started on her nurse's training?" Mrs. Weera boomed out to the clinic staff.

Shauzia didn't have the strength to protest. Did Mrs. Weera always get her own way?

The next day, Shauzia's head felt a little better, and she could open her eye wide enough to see the large cast on her leg.

"You've cracked some ribs," one of the nurses told her. "Your chest will be sore for awhile, but you'll mend. We were worried about your head, but you must have a thick skull. Nothing there seems damaged. You should see your face. It's all bruised."

"I hurt all over," Shauzia said. Since she didn't have a mirror, she didn't care what she looked like. "Can you give me something for the pain?"

"You'll have to live with it," the nurse said. "We're short of painkillers. We're short of everything. The pain will pass with time."

"Is my leg going to be all right?" Shauzia was almost afraid to hear the answer.

"You have a simple fracture. Six weeks in a cast and your leg will be mended."

"Six weeks!"

"Lower your voice, please. Do you have someplace else to be?"

"Of course I do. Do you think I want to be here?"

"I don't think any of us want to be here, yet here we are."

"Well, I don't have to stay here," Shauzia said flatly.

"No one's holding you prisoner," the nurse said, checking the bandages of the woman in the bed next to Shauzia.

"How can I walk with this bad leg?"

"Your leg is merely broken, not blown off. Stop complaining. You are luckier than most."

The nurse walked away then, so Shauzia couldn't talk back without yelling across the clinic. She would have done that if she hadn't felt too weak to shout.

"She must have been trained by Mrs. Weera," she mumbled.

"Try to be patient," the woman in the next bed said. She was more bandages than she was woman. They covered all of her face except for one eye. Her voice was old and raspy. "All things heal with patience."

"Patience just gets you more of what you've

already got," replied Shauzia. "Patience never heals anything. All patience does is make you forget you ever wanted anything better. Patience will turn you to stone."

"When all you have to choose between is patience or impatience, you'll find patience much easier on the mind."

"That's fine for you. You're old. You probably wouldn't do anything even if you could. I'm young. I have plans."

"How old are you?"

"Fourteen."

"I'm sixteen," the woman said.

For a long while, Shauzia didn't speak. Then she asked, "What happened to you?"

"A man threw acid in my face."

"Why did he do that?"

"He didn't like what I was doing. I thought I would be safe in a refugee camp, but I don't think there is a safe place for me anywhere."

"What were you doing that he didn't like?"

"I was teaching his daughter how to read."

"Was he Taliban?"

"Does it matter? Not all men with bad ideas belong to the Taliban. It hurts me to talk. Let me rest now."

Shauzia let her rest, and then she fell asleep herself.

When she woke up, the bed beside her was empty.

She grabbed the arm of a passing nurse.

"Where is she?" she asked, nodding at the bed.

"She didn't make it."

"You mean she died?"

"Let go of me."

"You don't care, do you? You don't even look sad that she died. You didn't do anything to help her!"

The nurse yanked herself free. "Do you know how many deaths we see here? How am I supposed to cry over all of them? All you do is lie there and complain. How dare you criticize me!"

"That's enough." An older nurse came over.

"What does she expect of us? There aren't enough bandages, not enough food, and not enough water." The nurse's voice rose in desperation. "Three more children died today. What sort of place is this? Farm animals are treated better."

"Stop it!" the older woman said sharply. "You're scaring the patients. Take a break and calm down. You're no use to me like this."

The young woman started to cry and ran off. The older nurse headed back to work.

Shauzia turned her head away. She didn't want to look at the empty bed.

The next day, she was given a pair of crutches. "Practice walking with them," the nurse told her, "but don't go far. Several other people have to use them today."

It felt great to be moving again, even though using the crutches was awkward. She walked a little bit away from the clinic and turned around to go back.

Then she stopped and looked at it instead.

The clinic was just one big tent, with the flaps open to allow what little breeze there was to flow through the tent. Cloth screens gave the patients in the beds some privacy, although not much, and kept some of the dust off them. On the edges of the clinic, families of the sick people sat on the ground, waiting for them to get well. Children cried. Nurses and doctors were busy with the line-up of people who had come to see them, cleaning and bandaging wounds and trying to comfort people crying with pain and sorrow.

No one was watching Shauzia to make sure she returned the crutches. She turned into a narrow, mud-walled street, and the clinic slipped out of sight behind her. She was getting out of this place.

First, though, she needed to find Jasper, who hadn't been allowed in the clinic. She'd make one last trip to the Widows' Compound, get her dog, and then leave without speaking to anyone.

No more Mrs. Weera. No more sick, desperate, crazy people. Just her, her dog and the great blue sea.

THIRTEEN

Shauzia made slow progress. Walking with crutches was hard. Sweat ran down the inside of her cast, making her leg itch and hurt at the same time. She half wanted to go back to her bed in the clinic, but she kept on.

"Boy, where are you walking to in this heat?" one of the men sitting at the side of the road called out as she walked by.

"Old man, what are you waiting for in this heat?" she asked in return.

"I am just waiting," the old man replied. "It is what I do. I don't remember what I am waiting for, but still, I wait. One day, you will wait like I do."

"Never!" Shauzia exclaimed.

"Already you are walking in the heat to get somewhere, but where can you go? There is nowhere but here. This street or that street, it is all the same. One day you will know this, and you will sit down and wait."

Shauzia walked away while the man was still talking.

She passed a lot of men like that, sitting and waiting, their eyes following her as she made her slow and awkward way down the road. The crutches were too short for her, and her back hurt as she stooped over to use them. She didn't speak to any more of the men. They didn't speak to her. They just watched, and waited.

Her leg was hurting very badly. She was hot and tired. She needed to get out of the sun and put her leg up.

She turned around to go back to the clinic, and realized she was totally lost.

She had been walking without noticing where she was going. The roads and pathways in the camp went in all sorts of directions. She hadn't been to this section when she'd run errands for Mrs. Weera. She had no idea where she was or how to get back.

She asked one of the sitting-and-waiting men where the Widows' Compound was. The man chewed the question over in his mind while Shauzia leaned impatiently on her crutches.

Another man came along. "What is happening?" he asked the first man.

"Boy wants to get to the Widows' Compound."

"Why do you want to do that, boy?"

The two men talking drew the attention of a third. Three men drew the attention of three more, and soon there were a dozen men in the little dirt street, debating the direction of the Widows' Compound, and even questioning whether there was a Widows' Compound.

"Why do you want to go there, boy?" someone asked her again. "Don't you know they started the food riot? You keep away from them. Women living together like that, they get up to no good."

The discussion switched to the food riot. The men said the widows had used a bomb to blow open the storehouse doors.

Shauzia used the opportunity to slip down a pathway, away from the men and their crazy stories.

She kept walking, turning this way and that, hoping to come upon something that looked familiar.

The mud walls came to an abrupt end, and Shauzia found herself looking out at an endless sea of tents.

It was the camp for new arrivals. Mrs. Weera had told her about it, but she had never seen it.

"There is no room for them in this camp, but they still come. Where else will they go? They arrive with nothing," Mrs. Weera said. "Some of them wait six months or more for a tent."

Shauzia turned around. This was neither the Widows' Compound, nor the way out of the camp.

The thought of heading back into the maze of mud walls made her turn around again. Maybe she could walk through the camp for new arrivals and find a faster way back to the Widows' Compound. The compass in her head told her that would be the right thing to do.

She waded into the new camp.

There were no roads or pathways that she could see. There was barely room to walk between the tents and, in some places, there was no room at all.

Some people had proper tents made of white canvas with UNHCR stamped on the side in big black letters. Some people had tents made out of rags stitched together. Some people had tents made from sheets of thin plastic stretched over sticks.

Shauzia poked her head into some of the tents. "Do you know where the Widows' Compound is?" she asked.

The people inside stared back at her with vacant eyes. The temperature inside the tents was even hotter than the temperature outside, but people were still crammed inside them. There wasn't really anyplace else to sit.

"Give me your crutches," a voice called out from a tent. Shauzia bent down and saw an old woman sitting inside. She was missing a leg. "Give me your crutches, so I can go away from here. I do not like this terrible place."

Shauzia hurried away. In her rush, she tripped on a tent peg and went sprawling onto the hard ground.

Children standing nearby laughed at her. Shauzia knew they were bored, and she was entertainment, but she was not in the mood to entertain anybody. She struck out at them with one of her crutches.

"That is no way to behave," a man said, helping her to her feet. "You are older than they are. You should show them how to be kind."

Shauzia hobbled away without thanking him.

She heard the noise of a truck and saw people rushing around carrying jugs and pans. Shauzia followed the crowd.

It was a water truck. The guards around it tried to get the people to line up, to wait their turn, but everyone was too thirsty. They crowded in around the truck.

Shauzia stayed on the edge of the crowd on top of a small rise in the ground and watched the scene below.

People who managed to fill their jugs with the precious water often saw most of it spill to the ground as they tried to get back through the crowd. One man had his whole jug knocked out of his hands, but when he tried to go back to the truck to have it refilled, he couldn't make his way through the mass of people. He waved his jug in frustration, hitting someone on the head. That man hit back, and soon a huge fight was underway.

Shauzia turned and walked away. She didn't want her other leg broken.

She found her way to the edge of the tents, to a rough bit of road. A white van, like the one aid agencies used, was coming toward her, so she stood in the middle of the road to stop it.

"I'm lost," she called out.

The aid worker got out of the van. "Where do you belong?" he asked.

"I belong at the sea!" Shauzia started to cry. "I belong in France! I belong in a field of purple flowers, where nothing smells bad, with no one screaming or pushing around me. That's where I belong."

The aid worker helped Shauzia into the passenger seat of the van and waited until she had stopped crying before he asked, "Where do you live now?"

Shauzia wiped the tears off her cheeks. "The Widows' Compound," she said.

They started to drive. The sea of tents and sad people seemed to go on forever.

"Who are they?" Shauzia asked.

"They've just left Afghanistan," the aid worker told her. "People are rushing to get across the border before the Americans attack."

"The Americans are going to attack?"

"They're angry about what happened in New York City."

"What happened?"

The aid worker kept one hand on the steering wheel while he fished around on the floor with his other.

"Here it is." He handed Shauzia a piece of newspaper he had found.

Shauzia looked at the photograph. Smoke poured out of the mangled remains of a building.

"Looks like Kabul," she said, letting the paper drop back to the floor.

She leaned her head against the window. The people they drove past did not look strong enough to blow up anything.

Then she closed her eyes and didn't open them again until they arrived at the Widows' Compound.

Her bed in the clinic had been given to someone else, Mrs. Weera told her. She set up a charpoy in some shade for Shauzia to rest on. Jasper sat on the ground below her, and the compound's children gathered around begging for stories until they were shooed away by Mrs. Weera so Shauzia could rest.

The next day there was an attack on the Widows' Compound. Half a dozen men tried to get over the walls, yelling that the women inside were immoral and should not be allowed to live together without men to watch over them.

Mrs. Weera and the other women beat the men back over the walls with brooms and anything else they could grab. Shauzia was stuck on the charpoy. Her crutches had been returned to the clinic, so she could do nothing but watch and yell at the men. Jasper, with his bark and his bared teeth, helped scare the intruders away.

Mrs. Weera had to hire extra guards. She didn't say so, but Shauzia knew she was worried about how she was going to pay for them.

Shauzia spent the next few weeks sitting with the women from the embroidery project. She hemmed napkins and tablecloths and waited for her leg to heal.

FOURTEEN

The Red Crescent nurse put down her cast cutters and pulled apart the cast.

Shauzia's leg looked scrawny and weak.

"Try to stand," the nurse said.

Shauzia carefully put some weight on the leg. It twinged a bit, but otherwise it felt all right. Jasper gave her newly freed leg a big sniff and a gentle lick.

"It was a simple break," the nurse said. "You were lucky. Stay away from riots from now on."

Shauzia took some more steps, trying out her mended leg.

"We'll have your first-aid kits ready this afternoon," the nurse said to Mrs. Weera, who had brought Shauzia to the clinic. "When are you leaving?"

"Tomorrow, I think. Or maybe tonight. I can't decide whether it's safer for us to travel after dark, or if we should wait until daylight."

"Both have risks," the nurse agreed.

"Where are you going?" Shauzia asked. Was she really about to be free of Mrs. Weera?

"Mrs. Weera is a very brave woman," the nurse said. "I hope you treat her with respect. She is taking several nurses back into Afghanistan."

"You're going back?" Shauzia almost yelled. "Why would you want to do that?"

"Our people are being bombed," Mrs. Weera replied quietly. "Thousands have gathered at the border, trying to get out, but the border has been closed. Nurses are needed."

"If the border is closed, how will you get in?"

"We'll have to sneak in, probably across the mountains."

"Just you women? You'll never get away with it. The Taliban will arrest you."

"We'll have to take that chance," Mrs. Weera told her. "People need us, and they'll help us as best as they can. We should get back to the compound now. I have lots to do."

The compound had been full of activity for the past week, but Shauzia hadn't paid too much attention to it. The embroidery group had switched from fancy needlework to cutting strips of material for bandages and patching the worn spots in old blankets. Shauzia had noticed all the rushing around, but she had not cared to ask about it.

That evening she sat on the ground, her back against the hut where she slept, and where the women's organization had their office. Women kept going in and coming out again. They paid no attention to her.

Farzana sat down beside her. Jasper thumped his tail and put his head in Farzana's lap.

"It's going to be awfully quiet without Mrs. Weera here," Farzana said.

"We'll still be able to hear her snoring at night. Even if she's on the other side of the world, her snores will reach us. She'll probably shatter the eardrums of all the Taliban soldiers, then take their place as ruler of Afghanistan."

"She'd have a whole country to boss around then," Farzana said with a giggle. "She'd like that."

"You think the Taliban has crazy laws? Mrs. Weera's would be even crazier. She'll force everyone to spend every afternoon playing field hockey."

Farzana laughed again. "She'll even make old people play, and the people on crutches."

"She's crazy!" Shauzia was angry now. She threw a stone across the courtyard, narrowly missing one of the busy women. "She's absolutely crazy to be going back into Afghanistan, especially without a man. She thinks she can make anything happen just because she wants it to happen. She's crazy!"

"What do you care?" Farzana asked. "You're going to the sea."

"That's right," Shauzia said. "Now that my cast is off, I'll be heading out."

"You're not taking me with you, are you?" Farzana asked.

Shauzia didn't reply.

"It's all right," Farzana said. "Mrs. Weera told me you wouldn't, but I already knew."

Shauzia didn't know what to say. She stroked Jasper's soft fur. She didn't like what she was feeling.

"So why do you just sit here?" Farzana asked. "Why don't you go?"

"I am going," Shauzia said. "I'm just resting first. It's a long way to the sea."

"Rest someplace else," Farzana said. "I

don't want to be around you right now."

"I was sitting here before you were."

"Do you have to have everything your way? I'm staying right where I am. You leave."

"All right, I'd be glad to." Shauzia got to her feet. "Just about anybody would be better company than you. Come on, Jasper."

Jasper rolled his brown eyes to look at her, but his head stayed in Farzana's lap.

"Stupid dog," Shauzia said, and she stalked off away from them.

She found a place to sit against the compound wall, where she didn't have to look at anyone. Then she took the magazine photo of France out of her pocket.

Maybe it was the dim evening light. Maybe it was her anger at Jasper for choosing Farzana over her. Whatever it was, for some reason the field of purple flowers didn't look so inviting anymore. In fact, it looked a little dull.

Shauzia put the picture back in her pocket and leaned against the wall. For a long while, she sat and thought.

"They're leaving! Mrs. Weera's leaving!"

Shauzia heard the call and got to her feet.

She had to see them leave. She had to make certain Mrs. Weera was well and truly going.

Everyone from the compound gathered in the courtyard to say goodbye. Shauzia hung back, watching, wanting to run away, but feeling compelled to stay.

Mrs. Weera sought her out. She wrapped Shauzia in one of her giant hugs.

"You are a precious, precious child," Mrs. Weera said softly. "I hope you get to the sea. I hope France welcomes you with open arms. They would be lucky to get you."

Mrs. Weera released her and joined her nurses. With one final wave, they left the compound.

The others drifted off to their homes. Shauzia, Farzana and Jasper stood in the doorway and watched the women walk away.

"They'd be so much safer if they had a man with them," Shauzia said.

"Or even a boy," Farzana said.

Without another thought, Shauzia sprang into action. She fetched her shoulder bag and blanket shawl from the hut. She stopped briefly where Farzana and Jasper were standing.

"Take care of Jasper," she said to Farzana.

"If the two of you get to the sea, give him a bath in the waves with this." She handed Farzana the bit of flowery soap from Tom and Barbara. Then she reached into her pocket, took out the photo of the lavender field, and gave that to Farzana, too.

Finally she bent down and hugged Jasper hard. She knew he wouldn't mind that she was crying.

Shauzia left the compound then, and headed off to meet Mrs. Weera and the nurses.

She had almost twenty years before she had to meet her friend Parvana at the top of the Eiffel Tower in Paris. She'd get there. But first she had a little job to do.

Mrs. Weera had long legs. Shauzia had to run to catch up to her.

AUTHOR'S NOTE

Afghanistan, a small country in central Asia, has been at war since 1978, when American-backed fighters opposed the Soviet-backed government. In 1980, the Soviet Union invaded Afghanistan, and the war escalated, with both sides bombing and killing with modern weapons.

After the Soviets left in 1989, a civil war erupted, as various groups fought for control of the country. The heads of some of these groups were known as war lords, and they were particularly brutal.

Into this mess came the Taliban. These were originally boys whose parents had been killed in the war with the Soviets. They were taken out of Afghanistan and trained in special military schools in Pakistan (funded by the Pakistan and American secret police) to form an army that would eventually take over the country. In September, 1996, the Taliban army took over the capital city of Kabul.

The Taliban imposed extremely restrictive laws, especially on girls and women. Schools for girls were closed down, women were no longer allowed to hold jobs, and strict dress codes were enforced. Books were burned, televisions smashed, music was forbidden, and a free press in any form became seriously illegal. The Taliban massacred thousands of their opponents and put others in prison. Some people simply disappeared, and their families may never know what happened to them.

The destruction of the war, and the meanness of the governments that grew out of the war, have created a huge refugee population, as Afghans fled their country for what they hoped was safety in Iran and Pakistan. Millions still live in huge refugee camps, or in slums in the cities. The war and terror have gone on so long that many people have spent their whole lives in these conditions.

Pakistan is a very poor country, and the huge influx of refugees has put a strain on the economy. Some Afghans were able to find work, but they often worked for criminally low wages, just to try to stay alive.

Although the Taliban are no longer in

power in Afghanistan, and many of the refugees have returned home, the decades of war have left the country in terrible shape. Bridges, roads and electrical plants have been destroyed. Few people in Afghanistan have clean water to drink. All the armies put land mines in farmers' fields, making it impossible to grow food there. As a result, many people die of hunger or from diseases caused by poor nutrition.

The greatest sign of hope for Afghanistan is that the schools have reopened, and all children – boys and girls – now have a chance to get an education. They have a chance, that is, if their families can afford to send them, if there is a school in their area, if there is a trained teacher to teach them, if there are books or even a piece of chalkboard for them to use. Another problem is that while life is getting back to normal in the capital city, many of the outlying provinces are still controlled by the war lords, and women and girls are again facing severe restrictions in those areas.

The terrible poverty and destruction in the country means the Afghan people need help from people around the world to rebuild schools, libraries, clinics and roads, and to provide basic supplies. To find out how you can help, you can contact the Libraries for Afghanistan Campaign at www.w4wafghan.ca.

Royalties from this book will be donated to Street Kids International, a non-profit organization that works with children around the world who are living on the streets. For more information, contact www.streetkids.org, or write to them at 38 Camden Street, Suite 201, Toronto, Ontario M5V 1V1.

Deborah Ellis
May, 2003

GLOSSARY

Badakhshan – A province of northeast Afghanistan.

burqa – A long, tent-like garment worn by women. It covers the entire body and has a narrow mesh screen over the eyes.

chador – A piece of cloth worn by women and girls to cover their hair and shoulders.

charpoy – A bed consisting of a frame strung with tapes or light rope.

Dari – One of the two main languages spoken in Afghanistan.

Genghis Khan – The Mongol conqueror (1162-1227) who formed a vast empire that stretched from China to Persia.

karachi – A cart on wheels pushed by hand, used to sell things in the market.

nan – Afghan bread. It can be flat, long or round.

Pashtu – One of the two main languages spoken in Afghanistan.

Red Crescent – The Muslim equivalent of the Red Cross, an international organization that provides aid to the sick and wounded in times of disaster and war.

roupee – Basic unit of money in Pakistan.

shalwar kameez – Long, loose shirt and trousers, worn by both men and women. A man's shalwar kameez is one color, with pockets in the side and on the chest. A woman's shalwar kameez has different colors and patterns and is sometimes elaborately embroidered or beaded.

Taliban – An Afghan army that took control of the capital city of Kabul in September, 1996, and was forced from power in the fall of 2001.

toshak – A narrow mattress used in many Afghan homes instead of chairs or beds.

UN – United Nations, an international organization that promotes peace, security and economic development.

UNHCR – United Nations High Commission on Refugees.

Uzbek – The language of the Uzbek people of central Asia.